N[ ]
folk tales
for children

NORFOLK FOLK TALES
FOR CHILDREN

Dave Tonge

Illustrated by Jim Kavanagh

For my own children, Joe & Sam.
Now full grown to manhood, but still
young'uns to me.

First published 2018

The History Press
The Mill, Brimscombe Port
Stroud, Gloucestershire, GL5 2QG
www.thehistorypress.co.uk

British Library Cataloguing in Publication Data.
A catalogue record for this book is available from the British Library.

ISBN 978 0 7509 8481 2

Typesetting and origination by The History Press
Printed and bound in Great Bristain by TJ International Ltd

Contents

About the Author and Illustrator

Dave was born and bred in Norfolk and goes by the name of the Yarnsmith of Norwich – although as a professional storyteller he travels all over England telling at museums, libraries, heritage sites, schools, festivals and fairs. He also loves history and thinks himself very lucky that he can dress up like a Saxon, Medieval or Tudor storyteller and tell tales in ancient castles and very old houses. From Hampton Court, one of Henry VIII's royal palaces, to William Shakespeare's boyhood home in Stratford-upon-Avon, all the way up to the Holy Island of Lindisfarne, the Yarnsmith wanders the roads bringing wonder wherever he goes.

Jim is an illustrator, storyteller and educator. He has illustrated numerous children's books, written plays, visited schools as an art, science and historical educator, worn all sorts of daft costumes and once painted an almost life-size pirate galleon on a playground. He has loved making the images for this book.

Introduction

Welcome young people (from now on known as young'uns) to my collection of Norfolk folk tales. Some of the stories take place only in Norfolk, home of the Broads, where wherries and other boats have sailed for many centuries, while others cross the county borders into Cambridgeshire and Suffolk. For along with Norfolk, they were part of the ancient Saxon Kingdom of the East Angles long ago.

Some stories cover the three counties, while others came from other countries long before they travelled to Norfolk in times past. Many people have settled in this place now called Norfolk: from the Beaker People of more than 4,500 years ago to the Romans, Saxons, Vikings and Normans. Then came Dutch and Flemish weavers in Tudor times, Italians after the Second World War and Congolese refugees from Africa today. Some of my own family came to Norfolk more than 100 years ago in search of work and decided to stay. Many people have settled in Norfolk over time – not just to take, but also to give. They have brought their ideas and beliefs, their customs, traditions and their stories, all of which have mixed and blended with what was here already, to make the folklore and folk tales of the county. They have become Norfolk tales, just by being told here over many generations.

The stories have also grown in the telling, although that does mean that some of them are a bit gruesome in places. But just remember that a story is just a story and cannot hurt you. And if you are still unsure, just imagine me or another storyteller telling the story to you and all should be well.

You should also know that when I tell stories I use a lot of old-fashioned words and I've included some of them in this book. But fear not, for I've also added a glossary, meaning a list of some of the stranger words. So if you don't know them already, you can find out what the words mean. Think of it as a quest, seeking out new words as well as stories!

You can also learn something about the history of Norfolk from this book, because each story is introduced with a fact about the county and its people. They are included here because these local events have helped change the stories from other lands into the Norfolk folk tales told today. I've also sorted my stories into five chapters, each one titled using dialect, meaning the words and sayings used by Norfolk people for hundreds of years. Some of those words, like some of the stories in my book, originally came from other lands, while others developed right here in Norfolk and might even go back to Saxon times! So young'uns, 'dew yew keep a troshin' – a Norfolk saying that has two meanings: Firstly, carry on with your good work, which in this case means reading my book. And secondly, look after yourselves.

Dave Tonge, 2018

Thank yous

Thanks to Helen James, Kimmy Voisey and Poppy Fee for proofreading my work. Also the young'un, Tal Fee, for his expert opinion on children's stories! Thanks also to Jim Kavanagh for his grand illustrations, and to Stewart Alexander, for what I borrowed from his version of the Pedlar of Swaffham. I'd also like to thank my mum for encouraging my imagination – she wrote about her childhood long ago and I've included my version of one of her stories here.

1

Slow yew down an' hold yew hard

'Slow yew down an' hold yew hard' is Norfolk dialect for 'slow down and wait a while'. I've used it as the title for this chapter about hale and hearty heroes because that's exactly what they didn't do! They all acted quickly when there was need. All except for Tom Hickathrift and John Chapman, who both needed a bit of a push.

Of the Lazy Lad and his Furious Fenland Fight

Many famous and heroic people have been born in Norfolk, including Horatio Nelson. He was a vice admiral in the Royal Navy and won many a victory during the Napoleonic wars, including the Battle of Trafalgar where he was killed in 1805. But there are other less well-known heroes from Norfolk, who never won great battles but showed strength and courage nonetheless. There was William Cullum, who grew up poor in Norwich more than 100 years ago. He called himself Billy Bluelight and was famous for racing the riverboats between Norwich and Yarmouth. There was also Robert Hales, the giant of Norfolk, who stood 7ft 8in tall and toured America.

But from a real Norfolk giant and real heroes like Nelson, to a fictional giant in the story of the hero Tom Hickathrift. Some think Tom's tale dates back more than 1,000 years and that it was inspired by the Viking god Thor, who did battle with many a giant. Tom's story is also like those of Jack the Giant Killer, whose own tales are similar to others from France and Norway. Tales that travelled here long ago – although not as fast as Billy Bluelight …

There was a time, young'uns, long ago, when men wore bright yellow caps upon their heads and hung great knives called seaxs from their belts. They were the Anglo-Saxons, who once called this land their home. And at that time there lived an old widow woman with her one and only son. His name was Tom Hickathrift, but everyone called him Idle Tom, for he was a lazy, lethargic lad who lay all day by the fire while eating his poor mother out of house and home. He feasted by the flames upon bread and pottage, while his poor old mother went without. And so it was that Tom grew big upon all his mother's hard work and home-cooked food. His shoulders were broad, so too his chest, while his arms were as thick as you young'uns' bodies and his hands were like two great spades used for digging the earth.

Tom grew so big that his poor mother could no longer afford to keep him and the old woman had to beg for all she needed. And one day she went to a nearby farm and asked the farmer if she might have some straw for her cow to rest upon. The farmer was not a kind man, yet still he said yes.

'But,' said the farmer, 'but,' said he, 'you can only take as much straw as your son Tom can carry.' For the farmer felt sure that Idle Tom would carry very little. The old woman begged Tom to collect the straw and after much nagging the lazy lad agreed. But only after he stopped on the way to pick up a long length of rope.

'Take as much as you can carry, Idle Tom', said the farmer as he laughed long, loud and lustily, for he felt sure that the lazy lad would carry very little. Tom took no notice. Instead he rolled out the rope and lay sheaf after sheaf of straw along it, until the great bundle of straw must have weighed a ton – and know, you young'uns, that a ton is very heavy indeed. 'Fool!' cried the farmer, 'Fool!' cried he. 'You will break your back with such a heavy load.' But by way of answer Tom swung the huge bundle onto his shoulder as if it were no more than a bagful of goose feathers, or perhaps a sackful of rags. And turning his back upon the farmer, Tom Hickathrift strode home.

News of Tom's strength travelled the land; he became famous throughout Norfolk, and even strange lands like Cambridgeshire and beyond. From that day on, all Tom's neighbours asked for the lusty lad's help with heavy work.

Once there was a forester, a man of the woods, who begged Tom's aid in moving a fallen tree. When Tom arrived, there were already twelve strong men struggling with rope and pulley, but so heavy was the tree that they could not move it, not even one inch – and that's about the thickness of my thumb. But then Tom took hold, grasping one end of the thick trunk with his thick arms and great hands. He lifted it into the air and lowered it gently onto a waiting cart. The forester was much pleased and offered Tom two shiny coins for his work, but the lusty lad would not take them. All that Tom wanted that day was some firewood for his mother's fire.

'Grant me,' said Tom to the forester, 'grant me,' said he, 'just a few twigs to keep my poor old mother warm at night.' And the grateful forester happily replied, 'Why yes, Tom, take all that you can carry.'

Well young'uns, you know what's coming next. Tom saw two more fallen trees even bigger than the one that lay upon the cart. He lifted one up upon his left shoulder and the other up upon his right, as if they were no more than a bagful of goose feathers, or perhaps a sackful of rags. And then turning his back upon the forester, Tom Hickathrift strode home.

News of Tom's strength spread even further across the land. Just as Shuck, whose story also appears in this book, travelled the highways and byways of East Anglia, so too Tom's fame roamed far and wide. He delighted in displaying his burly brawniness and fantastic feats for all to see – especially to girls, who all marvelled at his massive muscles and went 'oooh' and 'ahhh' and 'wow' every time Tom strode past! And so it was that Tom Hickathrift had many adventures – but none so fantastic as when he went to work for a beer brewer in King's Lynn.

The beer brewer wanted a strong man like Tom to carry his beer across the marshes to Wisbech, and he promised shiny coins to fill Tom's purse and food to fill his belly. He even promised the lusty lad a new suit of clothes, complete with hood, cloak and boots; and it cost the brewer dearly, for Tom was much bigger than all of you and even bigger than me, and I'm all grown up!

But the brewer did not care, for on the marshes around Wisbech there lived a great giant, who had killed and eaten all of the brewer's other servants. He had crunched their bones, sucked out all their marrow and washed down their lumpy bits with a barrel of the brewer's own beer. You think that's gruesome, young'uns, then perhaps you shouldn't read on. For the giant even hung their heads upon nearby branches, so that it looked like Wisbech marshes were covered in cruel Christmas trees! All were terrified of the monstrous, massive man and no one dared to travel the marsh path to Wisbech. Instead they rode their carts the long way, along the road that went around the marsh, but that added many miles to the journey and cost the beer brewer dear. So, that new suit of clothes was a small price to pay for Tom's help.

And help the lusty lad did. He flung open the gates leading to the ghastly giant's horrid home, and with his cart piled high with beer, Tom continued on his way.

It wasn't long before young Tom spied the giant and the giant spied him. The mammoth man fell upon the lad as the hungry fox falls upon a hen.

'Who dares take the path through my marsh?' roared the giant. 'Who dares?' roared he. 'Have you not heard what happens to all who stray too close to my land? I crunch their bones and suck out their marrow. I wash down their lumpy bits with the beer that they carry, and keep their heads to decorate my trees!' While others who'd heard the giant's words had screamed loudly – which, young'uns, was the last thing they ever did – Tom just laughed.

'I care not a fart for your threats, Giant,' said Tom, 'not a flying fart,' said he. The giant roared with anger, for no man before this day had ever answered him back.

'You are but a foolish child!' shouted the giant. 'A foolish child indeed!' shouted he. 'For you do not even have a weapon to fight me with, and I will crush you with my club.' And having spoken of his club, his own bloodstained beating stick, the giant went to fetch it.

It was true that Tom did not carry a weapon. Until this day his strong arms had served him well enough, but then he'd never met anyone

as large and as fierce as the giant. Tom looked
around, and seeing only his own cart piled
high with beer barrels nearby, he had an idea.
And when at last the giant returned with his
own cruel club, he was amazed to see Tom
holding one of the cartwheels in one hand and
the axle in the other. The wooden axle became
Tom's sword, the cartwheel became his shield,
and now he and the giant did battle.

The giant struck first, a mighty blow that would have felled a wayward wild pig, but Tom managed to knock it away with his cartwheel shield. In reply he struck the giant with the axle sword upon the shin – you know, young'uns, the bit at the front of your leg that really hurts if you hit it – and it hurt the giant too. He roared with pain as Tom struck him again, this time upon the head. The monstrous man swayed this way and that, as if already drunk from guzzling all of Tom's beer!

Tom and the giant rained down blow after blow upon each other for the rest of the day. First Tom, then the giant, taking turns beating each other with axle and club. For seven long days and nights the fight continued, until, on the morning of the eighth, Tom remembered the old saying: *you should always make hay while the sun is shining,* and this morning the sun shone bright. He beat the giant brutally, until at last the mean mammoth man roared no more, for he was very dead!

Next Tom went into the giant's cave to see what might be found, and what do you think was hidden there? That's right, TREASURE! Gold, silver and jewels and the lusty lad took it all. He tore down the cave and used the rock to build a fine house for his mother, and he drained the marshland and gave it to poor people to grow their crops. He also gave them some of the giant's treasure and the rest went to the church, for these were religious times. And know, young'uns, that from that day forward, no one ever called him Idle Tom again. From that day forward he was known to one and all as Mr Hickathrift!

Of the Boys with Bare Backsides

In 1914 a strike started in the small village of Burston in Norfolk, led by children who refused to go to the parish school. They were striking because their teachers, Tom and Annie Higdon, had been sacked, thrown out because the school managers did not approve of their support for unions that helped poor farm workers living nearby. The children marched around the village, making noise and waving flags. They had the support of their parents and also large unions and so were able to raise money to build their own strike school on the village green. The strike lasted for twenty-five years and even when it was over, the strike school was used for another twenty years after that.

The events of 1914 show us that children did speak their mind long ago and that was also true even further back in Tudor times. In 1549, Kett's Rebellion took place in Norfolk, with poor people protesting about many things, including enclosure – where common land, once used by all, was fenced off by landowners. Poor farmers near Wymondham began knocking down the fences of a landowner called Robert Kett, who for some reason agreed with the rioters and led them to Norwich; an important city in

Tudor times. But it didn't go well for Kett and his poor followers, although to know more of that you must read the folk tale below.

The country gnoffes, Hob, Dick and Hick
with clubs and clouted shoon
Shall fill the vale of Dussin's Dale
with slaughtered bodies soon

This rhyme is a piece of folklore, young'uns, an ancient prophecy about Kett's uprising that is supposed to be older than the rebellion itself.

29

The 'country gnoffes' were the poor people, who thought that it would be their enemy's bodies that would fill the vale of Dussin's Dale, although in truth, it would be the poor protesters who died that summer long ago. But there are other folk tales linked to the events of 1549, about half-naked boys baring their backsides! So in honour of the old prophecy of Hob, Dick and Hick, I have set those stories down here in like fashion, writ as rhymes:

Now listen young'uns, what e're your age
to a tale of some poor boys
For children would be heard sometimes
they too could make some noise

When Robert Kett and his men
camped out on Mousehold Heath
The Norwich gates were closed to them
thinking them vagabonds and thieves

And so Robert's men attacked the gates
with club and stave and stick
But the Norwich people they shot back
with bows and arrows thick

The arrows they shot through the air
all fell upon Kett's men
But amid their ranks were half-naked boys
some aged less than ten

They ran among the arrows
and gathered them up quick
They pulled them from their bodies
where some arrows they did stick

The ragged boys with bare backsides
gave the arrows to Kett's men
Who set them to their own yew bows
and shot them back again

And so Kett captured Norwich
for a short while anyway

31

But of bare buttocked boys we are not done
one yet has more to say

To Mousehold Heath Kett's men returned
and there they all did wait
Until to Norwich, Warwick came
an Earl, poor men did hate

He sent his herald to meet with Kett
to try and end the fight
He tried to make peace with Kett
But not all there thought it right

Although he promised pardons
that Kett's men would go free
No one trusted Warwick's man
he lied for all to see

And so one boy among them
pulled his ragged trousers down
He bared his backside at Warwick's man
who did scowl and did frown

The herald he left Mousehold
so angry at the lad
And though Kett's men all laughed and cheered
the ending would be bad

My poem is about some boys
who long back bared their bums
I hope it made you laugh a bit
I hope you found it fun

But just remember what happened next
when the herald wore a frown
His men with bows and arrows
shot the bare arsed boy straight down

And just remember what happened next
when to Dussin's Dale Kett came
For Warwick's army followed close behind
there to kill and maim

And just remember the prophecy
a rhyme that is old

33

I write it here again for you
a lesson to behold:

**The country gnoffes, Hob, Dick and Hick
with clubs and clouted shoon
Shall fill the vale of Dussin's Dale
with slaughtered bodies soon**

Over 3,000 men died that day
and many more were caught
They were hanged from tree and castle
a hard lesson they were taught

Of the Poor Pedlar and his Wondrous Walk to Wealth

One of the most famous heroes of Norfolk was Boudicca, the warrior queen of the Iron Age Iceni tribe who rebelled against Roman rule nearly 2,000 years ago. Many think that Iron Age people were primitive and savage, but that's not true. They made beautiful torcs

– gold and silver neck rings – many of which have been found at Snettisham in Norfolk. Some have been pulled out of the ground by farmers ploughing and others by metal detectorists, looking for treasure. It seems that the Iceni buried them there long ago to protect them from the Romans and other Iron Age tribes. We know that some of the finer treasure was buried beneath scraps of gold and silver with earth in between, perhaps in the hope that anyone finding the scraps would not guess that there was even more treasure below. All of which reminds me of the story of the poor pedlar from Swaffham in Norfolk – a tale that is also about treasure buried beneath treasure!

Before I tell it though, you should know that although some of my family come from far away, my mother's mother came from Swaffham 100 years ago. But much earlier still, in late medieval times, a man called John Chapman also lived there, and paid for the rebuilding of part of

Swaffham church. John seems to have gotten very rich very quickly, and the story set down below was told to explain his sudden wealth. In truth though, the story is not John's, for there is also an older Jewish version of this Norfolk folk tale and others from Ireland, Austria and even ancient Persia. Just as the Romans came here and conquered the Iron Age tribes long ago, so too stories came here and we made them our own. They are now Norfolk treasures and as valuable as any golden torc …

If one day, young'uns, you find yourself in Swaffham church, you might see a small wooden carving of a pedlar with a pack upon his back. And if you have no idea what a pedlar is, know that long ago you didn't go to the shops, for the shops came to you. Pedlars walked the land with a pack upon their back, travelling in all weathers, along rutted rain-soaked roads, frostbitten pathways and dry dusty tracks, calling their wares – meaning the things that they sold from their packs – shouting out

loudly, 'What do you lack, what do you lack, what will you buy from the pack on my back?' And in their pack they sold pots, potions and pins, buttons, buckles and bells. But this is not a tale about all pedlars long ago, oh no. It is the story of just one, John Chapman, the pedlar of Swaffham. The carving in the church is of him and this is his story set down below.

John and his family lived in a mean cottage on the edge of the town. But I do not say that it was a nasty place, young'uns, only that it was small and cramped, for that was what 'mean' meant long ago. For John never sold much of his wares – not pots, potions or pins, nor buttons, buckles or bells – and so he was very poor. So poor that his family all slept in one bed, just as my mother Mary and her sisters did in another tale in this book. And John only had one stool and a wonky bench in his mean house and his family had to take turns sitting down! There was a hole in the roof as big as my head, where the rain poured in upon the hard earth floor, for know that John could not afford carpets, or even floorboards to lay them on. John's door was hanging from its hinges and there was no glass in the windows, for glass was very expensive long ago. Instead John and his family had to make do with wooden shutters in the windows, which squeaked and squealed on their rusty hinges whenever Mother Winter's wicked winds blew hard.

And often the winds did bellow across the flat, bare lands where John lived. Often Mother Winter wrapped herself around his family like an icy cloak and her frostbitten fingers reached deep inside them, tickling their ribs. And if you've ever had your ribs tickled by Mother Winter, young'uns, you'll know it's not that nice at all! And so it was that each night, John and his family would shiver in their one bed with only thin blankets to cover their lean hungry bodies and torn curtains that hung around the bed to keep Mother Winter away. Each night they lay shivering and dreamt of summer when all would be warm and their small garden would bloom. For each summer, bees buzzed and birds sang in their small garden, which blossomed with flowers, fruit, veg and an apple tree. It was an old tree, but every late summer the branches bent low with rosy red apples that were big and sweet to eat. Some were nearly the size of my head, but not quite big enough to block the hole in John's roof!

39

Well, winter and summer and spring and autumn too, John Chapman travelled the highways and byways, the trackways and pathways; calling his wares, selling pots, potions and pins and buttons, buckles and bells to anyone who would buy them. However, few bought John's wares and every night he returned home, tired and feeling low, and this night John was so worn out that he went straight to bed and quickly fell asleep. But no sooner did John Chapman fall asleep than he had a strange dream, for in his dream a voice spoke to him. It said 'John Chapman, John Chapman. Go to London Bridge, for there you will hear good news!'

John awoke and thought, 'Go to London? I can't go to London, for London is a long, long way away from here. And besides,' thought John, 'dreams are silly, dreams are sad, dreams are for fools. You shouldn't take any notice of your dreams.'

Well, what say you, young'uns? Do you think that the pedlar of Swaffham was right, or do you think that he was wrong? Should you take notice of the weird and wonderful whimsy that comes to us all when we're asleep? We shall see soon enough, for night after long night, John Chapman had the same strange dream telling him to go to London, for there he would hear good news. And after a week of being kept awake, he thought, 'I have no choice. I must go to London Bridge in search of the good news that the dream said I would have.' John packed his pack with bread, cheese, some of his red rosy apples and also a flask of ale. He kissed his wife and children sweetly, wiped away their tears and set off on the road to London.

But know that London was a long, long way away from Swaffham in Norfolk and so John walked and he walked then he walked some more. John slept beneath hedges and even in a ditch when he could find nowhere else to lay his weary head. For seven days he walked until finally he made it to London. In those days long ago it was surrounded by a large stone wall with many gates where packhorses, wagons and people like John passed through every day, to see the sights and sell their wares. John, though, had nothing to sell. Instead he went straight to London Bridge that crossed the River Thames. Now I'm sure some of you young'uns have been to London and seen London Bridge. I'm sure that you all think that it's a good bridge, and it is in many ways. But London Bridge long ago was even better, for it had houses and shops upon it and a gate at each end. And sometimes the heads of wrong doers were stuck on poles

above the gates, looking down upon all those who passed beneath! John Chapman walked onto London Bridge, making sure that he did not look up at the heads looking down on him while also holding his nose, for the River Thames was like one great toilet for all those who lived in the great city long ago!

John Chapman found a gap between two houses and sat down, while everyone else upon the bridge that day went about their busy business. None paid any attention to the poor pedlar squatting low close by. John crossed his arms, crossed his legs and waited for the good news that the dream said he would have, but no good news came to him. All day long he waited, until the sun went down, the moon took over and John paid a penny for a bed in an inn that stood close by.

The following day John returned to London Bridge. He found a gap between two houses and sat down, while everyone else upon the bridge that day went about their busy business.

None paid any attention to the poor pedlar squatting low close by. John crossed his arms, he crossed his legs and he waited for the good news that the dream said he would have, but no good news came to him. All day long he waited, until the sun went down, the moon took over and John paid a penny for a bed in an inn that stood close by.

Well, what say you, young'uns? Was John wrong to have taken notice of his dreams? Before you decide, remember my story is not yet at an end …

For five full days John sat on London Bridge and waited for the good news that his dream had promised, but no good news came to the poor pedlar. He was out of pennies and so packed his pack to return home. But John was as sad as he was tired and poor, for he feared that his wife and children would be woeful and that his friends would all laugh at him for believing his dreams. But as John packed his pack for the long journey home, a glover came out of his shop to talk to him – a man who made fancy gloves for fancy people's fancy hands. For know that all posh folk wore gloves long ago and that William Shakespeare's father was a glover in Stratford in Tudor times. Perhaps Will would have been one too if he, like John Chapman, had not gone to London long ago to seek his fortune. But enough of Shakespeare, for the glover spoke to John asking him what his business was upon London Bridge. ''Ere,' said the glover in a Londony sort of way, ''ere,' said he, 'what you doin' on my bridge? For I've been watchin' you for five days and you ain't bought nuffin, you ain't sold nuffin and you ain't even been beggin'. So what you doin' on my bridge?'

Well, John Chapman told the glover of his tale, the very same story that I've just told all of you. Of the dream telling him to go to London Bridge, for there he would hear good news. And when he finished, the glover laughed long, loud and lustily in a Londony sort of way.

For he went, 'Nah, nah, nah, nah, naaaah! You mean to tell me,' said the glover, 'you mean to tell me,' said he, 'that you came all the way to London just because you had a dream?' Again the glover laughed long, loud and lustily and told John Chapman that he was a foolish fellow for taking notice of his dreams. 'Don't ya know,' said the glover, 'don't ya know,' says he, 'dreams are silly, dreams are sad, dreams are for fools. You shouldn't take no notice of your dreams.' And now the glover told John that he had had a dream just last night and that in his dream he didn't live and work on London Bridge, for in his dream he lived in a small cottage in a far off place called Swashham, Swishham, or something like that. He told John of how he dreamt that he lived in a mean house with just one bed and only one stool and a wonky bench to sit upon. He told John that there was a hole in the roof as big as his head, and said that the door was hanging from its hinges and there were only wooden shutters in the windows, which squeaked and squealed on their rusty hinges whenever Mother Winter's wicked winds blew hard. 'But in my dream,' said the glover, 'in my dream,' said he, 'I had a garden, and in that garden was an apple tree. And in my dream,' said the glover, 'I had a spade and I dug at the roots of the apple tree and I found gold,' said he. 'But if you think that I'm goin' to go walkin' across the land in search of an apple tree just because I had a dream, you must be even more foolish than I thought.'

But John Chapman did not reply to the glover, for John Chapman was no longer there. If it took him seven days to walk from Swaffham to London, it only took John three days to run all the way back! And I'm sure you young'uns know what happened next.

John embraced his family, kissed them sweetly and got a spade. Then he went to his apple tree and he dug and he dug and he dug some more until finally his spade struck something hard. John cleared the earth away and there was a box. He lifted it out of the hole, brought the spade down hard upon the lock and slowly, oh so very slowly, he lifted the lid. Now at this point, young'uns, you must imagine the sound of a creaky lid, or even make the sound out loud if you wish. And when you've done that, imagine gold, silver and jewels sparkling brightly, for that was what was in the box. John Chapman, the pedlar of Swaffham, was rich beyond his wildest dreams – and you can't get much richer than that! But he was a kind man and shared his treasure with the whole town and even paid to rebuild the church. He also built a great house of brick and stone, with glass in the windows, for his family to live in, and his wife and children all had seats of their own! John would also hold fine feasts for his friends and neighbours where he would tell the tale that I have just told all of you – a tale that he would always end like this: 'Always, always, always follow your dreams. You must always follow your dreams!'

Except, young'uns, that's not really the end of the story, for I have two more things to tell.

Firstly, there is another story in my book about some pilgrims who also had a dream, but I do not think that they would agree with John Chapman's last words. Seek out their story if you haven't already and you'll find out why not. And secondly, John's tale does not really end there, for in another version he also found a small tablet with the treasure chest, upon which were written strange words. It was the language of Latin that John did not know and so he put it aside and it was almost forgotten until one day, a priest was passing who could read the weird words. And this is what the tablet said: 'Under me lies another much richer than I.' The priest told John what it said and he needed no further telling. Again the pedlar of Swaffham dug and he dug in the same spot he had dug long before, and found a huge pot of gold hidden much deeper still!

Well there my tale finally ends
a Norfolk treasure for you to keep
One of many versions from many lands
its beginnings buried deep

Of the Soldier, Sovereign and Saint

There is a village in Norfolk called Heacham where it is said the Native American princess Pocahontas once stayed when she came to Britain more than 400 years ago. She was famous for having helped stop the fighting between her tribe and the English, but hers is a sad tale, for she died in England before she could return to her beloved homeland.

She is not the only royal person from another land who came to a sad end here, for the next tale involves the death of the Danish King, Ragnar. It's also about Saint Edmund, king of the East Angles, one of the seven Saxon kingdoms and the one that gives the English their name – the Angles became the English.

Some say that Edmund came over here as a boy, landing on the Norfolk coast at Hunstanton. That may be true, but remember that folk tales can't always be trusted, for they borrow from stories from other lands. Edmund was martyred, meaning killed for his beliefs, but his tale is much like that of Saint Sebastian from Italy, who was attacked in exactly the same way as the English king. There is also the story of Mary of Egypt, whose head was guarded by a lion. But to know how her story fits in with Edmund's tale, you must read on …

There are many brave heroes known to the English, young'uns, including St George, the patron saint of England, although like many of the tales in this book, his also comes from another land long ago. There is, however, another hero who once lived right here in East Anglia and in this place we now call Norfolk: a hero called King Edmund, although like all folk tales his is a story made up of a tiny bit of truth wrapped up in a whole lot of lies. Edmund was a real warrior king who became a saint and wanted only peace. But it is the way of things, that while there are those who crave only friendship with their neighbours, others want only war. And so to my tale that doesn't start here in Norfolk – instead it starts far away in the land of the Danish Vikings long ago.

For there was once a king of Denmark called Ragnar Lodbrok, a strange sounding name to some of you perhaps and in truth it was. For Lodbrok means 'hairy trousers' in English, and Ragnar won his name by killing and skinning a stag to make himself some trousers, which he painted with hot pitch to make them hard. Ragnar's hairy trousers became like armour, the hair like thick iron nails, and all this he did to win a wife. Thora was her name and Ragnar Lodbrok wished to wed her, but she was guarded by a wyrm, meaning a dragon of sorts. It was much like another wyrm who sleeps soundly somewhere else in this book and what the Scandinavian peoples of Denmark, Norway and Sweden called a lindworm; a cruel creature with ferocious, fearsome fangs and a poisonous bite. Many warriors had died trying to save fair Thora, but not Ragnar Lodbrok. The serpent wrapped itself about him and with fearsome fangs tried to bite deep. But the pointy, pitch-hard hair of the Viking king's trousers pierced the serpents inner mouth as Ragnar's sword came down hard upon its skull, killing the wicked wyrm dead.

And so it was that Ragnar married Thora and they had two sons called Ingvar and Ubba, whom he loved dearly, although it was said that he loved hunting even more. Ragnar would often go a-hawking – to catch duck and other waterfowl with his favourite falcon. But one day the bird swooped down upon a goose that was too big for it to kill and both birds spun and twirled hard and heavy in the air, falling down, down, down into the sea. Well, young'uns, Ragnar Lodbrok loved his sons, but it is said he loved his falcon even more and he quickly launched a small boat into the sea to rescue his favourite bird of prey. But quicker still a storm rose up and swept Ragnar's small boat out to sea, while his men wailed woefully from the beach, weeping bitter tears for the loss of their brave and powerful king.

For many days and many nights Ragnar was tossed upon violent waves until at last he was washed ashore at Reedham in Norfolk, now inland, but much closer to the coast when this tale was first told long ago. The Viking king was discovered by Saxons, dying in the bottom of his small boat. Just as we are suspicious of strangers now, so too they were wary of people that they did know, long ago. And so it was, the Saxons took him prisoner and brought him before their king, Edmund, whose tale is yet to be told. Edmund was impressed by Ragnar, and he in turn grew to like the English king. Although their peoples were enemies at this time, they became firm friends. And even though Ragnar was in truth Edmund's prisoner he allowed the Viking leader many freedoms, including the right to hunt on Saxon lands. For Ragnar Lodbrok loved to hunt and hunting loved him, by which I mean that he was good at it. He was even better than Edmund's chief huntsman Bern, who until Ragnar came to this land was the best of all Edmund's hunters and praised for his skill by all.

55

So great was Ragnar's skill at hunting, be it hawking with birds of prey, or riding down wild boar with lance and bow, that Bern grew jealous of how everyone sung Ragnar's praises, where once they had sung only his. Bern's jealousy became a rampaging rage and one day he tricked Ragnar into the woods, telling him that there was a great stag that they both could hunt. But then the savage Saxon, Bern, struck Ragnar down with an oaken log, killing him dead and burying the Viking's body beneath leaf, twig and dirt, so that none would know of his dreadful deed. But one of Edmund's hunting hounds had become Ragnar's firm friend. For dogs can be the most faithful of companions to man, as you'll find out if you read the story of Old Shuck, who also roams the pages of this book. So faithful a friend was Ragnar's dog that he led Edmund's men to the dead Viking's body and cowered and shivered whenever Bern came close by.

And so it was that Bern was taken prisoner and found guilty of his cruel, callous crime. And King Edmund had the huntsman cast into the sea in the very boat that had brought Ragnar to this land months before. For Edmund thought that while Ragnar was an innocent man and so passed safely across the sea, Bern was guilty of murder and so would surely drown. It would be in God's hands – he would choose what happened to Bern, or so they believed long ago. Know, young'uns, that Bern survived. Now whether it was God, or just good weather, I cannot say; you must make up your own mind about that. Whatever the reason, Bern washed up on the shores of Ragnar's Danish kingdom and his men recognised the boat that had taken their lord from them so many months ago. They dragged Bern to the halls of Ragnar's children, Ingvar and Ubba, who still mourned the loss of their father – their tears were still fresh upon their faces. Seeing their grief and sadness, Bern saw a chance for revenge against his old master King Edmund, and now lies and false fables fell from between his treacherous teeth. Bern told the two brothers that it was Edmund who had had their father cruelly killed and that he, Bern, had sailed to Denmark to tell them of Edmund's dark and deadly deed.

Ingvar and Ubba's anger knew no bounds – red-faced and roaring, they attacked East Anglia with more than 20,000 men, pillaging and plundering the coast and maiming and murdering many, while stealing from all those that they killed. King Edmund's army fought bravely against the attackers, but the Danes were too many and Edmund was trapped in one of his castles. The Saxons were besieged with little to eat, but Edmund was a cunning and clever king and had an idea to trick his Viking enemies. He ordered that an old bull be fed upon the last of their grain so that it grew fat and swollen. The bull was then released from the castle and the Danes shot it down with many arrows, for they too had empty bellies. But when they cut the dead beast open and all the grain spilt out from its belly they were amazed but also angry. If Edmund had grain enough to fill and fatten just one bull, then he must have grain enough to feed his soldiers for months to come – they would never be starved out of the castle.

The Danes went home, but the following year they returned with even more soldiers, which Ingvar and Ubba divided in two. Ubba and his Viking warriors travelled into Cambridgeshire, where they maimed and murdered many more Saxons. Ingvar took his soldiers to Thetford in the west of Norfolk to rest a while before he battled Edmund and his men. Now you should know, young'uns, that there are some as say that Ingvar continued to Hoxne at the very top of

Suffolk where King Edmund had his court. But there are others who tell in folk tale at least that he went to Hellesdon in Norfolk. Wherever Ingvar went, north or south, a great battle took place between King Edmund's fearless forces and Ingvar's mettlesome men. So fierce was the fighting that many men on both sides were killed and their bones littered the land for many years to come. And perhaps King Edmund's army would have won the day had not Ubba and his soldiers come to his brother Ingvar's aid. And so it was that Edmund had no choice but to surrender himself to the Viking brothers, to save the rest of his men.

But Ingvar and Ubba did not treat Edmund well. Thinking that it was he who had killed their father Ragnar, they had the Saxon king beaten with wood and tied fast to a tree. Know also that the Vikings were pagans at this time and did not follow the Christian God as Edmund did. Yet no matter how much the Danes dealt Edmund bitter blows upon his broken body, still he called to his God. And so it was they shot arrow after arrow into Edmund's body until he looked more like a misshapen hedgehog than a noble upright man, and he died upon that tree. But still the vicious Vikings were not done, for they cut off Edmund's head. They kicked it here and there, like a ghastly game of football, before throwing it into some twisted and tangled trees, where they thought that it would never be found.

Eventually the Vikings left and Edmund's faithful men came in search of their king. They pulled the many arrows from his bloodstained body and carried it away, while others stayed behind and searched for his missing head. They looked here, there and everywhere, but the head could not be found. Still they would not give up until at last they heard the howling of a wolf far away. Closer and closer the Saxons crept towards the baying beast, full of fear, for wolves could be cruel creatures. But this was no wicked wolf as its howls were replaced with the cries of their dead king, Edmund. 'Here,' he called, 'here, here,' called he. Following his voice, the Saxons found his severed head laying between the paws of a great shaggy wolf who was guarding it until they came close by. And only when Edmund's warriors took up the head of their king, did the wolf get up and slowly walk away.

Of my tale, young'uns, there is little more to tell, save only that when the king's head was placed by his lifeless body, the two were joined and became as one once more. It was called a miracle by all who saw it, one of many miracles, or so the storytellers of old did say. Some told of how his hair and fingernails continued to grow long after Edmund was dead, and that his body did not wither and waste away. Others spoke of how all those who visited his tomb were cured of sickness and disease. It was also told of how once his ghost appeared to another Viking king called Sweyn, and such was his terror at seeing the phantom King Edmund, that the Viking died right there upon the road!

Make of that what you will, but remember young'uns, whether or not you believe this tale, they did think it true long ago. And know that King Edmund was the patron saint of England, long before St George took his place.

2

H'yer fa got a dickey bor?

'H'yer fa got a dickey bor?' is Norfolk dialect for 'has your father got a donkey neighbour?' I've used it as the title for this chapter because the traditional answer to the question is, 'Yis, an' he want a fule ter roid 'im, will yew cum?' which means, 'Yes, and he wants a fool to ride him, will you come?' It's a reply well suited to the next three stories, because there are foolish, fickle folk in all of them.

Of the Petty Pilgrims and the Measly Meat Pie

Norfolk was once well known for its religious shrines – places where medieval people went to visit the graves of saints and religious objects too, in the hope that they would be cured of sickness, or helped in some other way. There was the shrine of St Walstan's that healed sick farm animals as well as people. Also the Sword of Winfarthing church that was said to make any woman who kissed it pregnant with a baby. But most famous of all was the Shrine of Our Lady at Walsingham. Nearly 1,000 years ago a noblewoman saw a vision of Mary, the mother of Jesus, at Walsingham and that's why the shrine was built. It was so famous that people came on pilgrimage there, meaning that they travelled from all over England and other lands, too. Even King Henry VIII visited Walsingham just before his Reformation, when England changed from a Catholic to a Protestant country and all the shrines were destroyed.

But now the shrine has been rebuilt and once again pilgrims journey there from all over the world, just as the pilgrims in the next story were on pilgrimage to Walsingham, although long ago. But the story itself has also been on a journey, for it started out as an Islamic tale, told by Muslims in many lands from Egypt to India. Not surprising when you know that many of the Christian pilgrims who visited Walsingham also went on pilgrimage to the Holy Land, where they would have mixed with Muslims long ago …

Here's a funny tale for you young'uns, of greed and boastful ways. For sometimes even religious folk long ago thought only of themselves. I say this because once there were three pilgrims on a pilgrimage to Walsingham long ago. They preached and prayed to all who would listen upon the road. They taught poor children to read their letters wherever they stopped to rest. They cared for the sick and the needy in all the places they passed by. And all they asked in return was a bed for the night and food to fill their bellies before they continued on their way. But times were hard and all the three pilgrims got this day was a measly meat pie. It was too small to fill the bellies of three well-fed pilgrims, and all three looked upon the mini morsel with envious, jealous eyes, while each in turn argued why it should be he alone who should enjoy the modest meal.

The first of the three pilgrims said that the measly meat pie should be his, because he was the most religious of all three of them. He was always at prayer and taught all he met upon the road of God in Heaven and the Devil in Hell.

But the second pilgrim said that he should tuck into the tiny, tasty pastry, because he was a clever man. He knew of numbers and letters and taught all he met upon the road of words and the world's many wonders.

But the third pilgrim also thought that the puny pastie should be his to chew, because he was skilled in the ways of medicine. He cured all he met upon the road of their boils and their bellyaches, their sorrows and their sores.

Each of the three pilgrims had good claim to the paltry pie that lay before them and with their bellies barking loudly, they argued into the night. None would give way to the others, until finally hunger gave way to tiredness and all three wished to sleep as much as they longed for the meaty treat. And so it was that the third of the three pilgrims said that they should sleep upon their quarrel, and that the pie would make one of them a fine breakfast. 'For,' said the pilgrim, 'for,' said he, 'in the morning we will each tell the others our dreams, and the one whose is most religious in spirit and deed shall receive the measly meat pie.' In other words, young'uns, he whose dream was most pious would win the pie (you might need to check the glossary to get that joke!).

The other pilgrims agreed and soon all three were sleeping soundly. But early the following morning all three were wide awake, thinking once more about the measly meat pie. And so it was, the first of the three pilgrims told of his nasty and nightmarish dream – of how he was awoken by the creaking and cracking of stone and the snapping of tree root; of how the earth had opened before him and he had fallen, down, down, down, into the deep, dark crevices of Hell. The pilgrim said that in his dream he had fought long and hard with demons and choked upon sulphur and smoke. 'And then,' said the pilgrim, 'then,' said he, 'I came face to face with the Devil himself, but so strong was my religion, that the Devil was more scared of me than I was scared of him, and he threw me back up to the world above.'

Well, young'uns, that's a strange and dreadful dream is it not? Yet the second pilgrim's dream was even stranger still. He dreamt of how he was awoken by angels singing sweetly in the night sky above and of how in his dream the pilgrim climbed a staircase higher and higher and higher into the heavens high above. He told of how he plucked upon a harp while angels danced all about him. 'And then,' said

71

the second pilgrim, 'then,' said he, 'I came face to face with God, the maker and master of all things and so strong was my religion that God saw that I would serve him better on earth than in the heavens and so he threw me back down to the world below.'

It was now time for the third pilgrim to tell of his dream, but he had no dream to tell. 'Alas,' said the pilgrim, 'alas,' said he, 'I did not dream last night, because I could not sleep.' And he told the other two of how he was kept awake all night by the creaking and cracking of stone, the snapping of tree root and the sweet, sweet song of the angels in the heavens above. He told of how he opened his eyes and saw the first pilgrim falling into Hell, while the second climbed a staircase into the heavens above. 'And so,' said the third pilgrim, 'so,' said he, 'thinking that I would never see either of you again, I ate that measly meat pie all up.' And so he had – every last crumb!

Well, young'uns, in the tale of the pedlar of Swaffham, also in my book, we learn that it's a good idea to follow your dreams. But I'm not so sure that the first two pilgrims in this tale would agree!

Of the Foolish Friars and the Brawl that Brought them Low

In 1272, a fight broke out between the people of Norwich and the monks of the city's cathedral about who controlled the Tombland market. The gates of the cathedral were closed and the prior, meaning the monk in charge, led other monks against the rioters with 'fire and sword'. But the people of Norwich were just as bad, burning the cathedral gates and destroying many of the buildings within its grounds. As part of their punishment the people were forced to pay for the gates to be rebuilt and they never forgot the monks' greed. But the same was true all over the country, as many people believed that monks and also friars were greedy grasping people who only cared about themselves. That's why they told stories about bad monks and friars like the one set down below.

The tale also tells of Sir Thomas Erpingham, a real knight who fought at the Battle of Agincourt and was mentioned by William Shakespeare in his play *Henry V*. Shakespeare was a storyteller who adapted tales from other lands and the same is true of all storytellers and their tales, for the next story is very similar to others from France, Germany and Italy. And all of them were just as silly as this one …

Some people think that young'uns like all of you are foolish and don't listen, not thinking before you act. But what's true of some of you is also true of grown-ups like me. Know that adults can also behave in strange and reckless ways, especially when they are in love! Now I know that many of you do not like talking about love. I know that some of you girls hate boys and some of you boys hate girls, but one day you might just fall in love! Perhaps you'll be walking down the road and a boy or girl will give you their eye. Not give you their actual eye, for that would be weird and a bit messy too! I simply mean that they'll look at you in a special way that will make you feel dizzy and delighted at the same time. Love can make even the wisest person foolish and even the most serious man or woman silly, which is why this foolish story is made sillier still by my bad rhymes:

> There was an old knight long ago
> Thomas Erpingham was his name
> He loved his wife Joan very much
> and she loved him just the same
>
> They would kiss, coo and cuddle
> as grown-ups often do
> They would call each other silly names
> like Chick and Sausage and Boo

75

But grown-ups are bewildering folk
like you they break the rules
A friar called John, he loved Joan too
and love it makes men fools

For Friar John wrote sweet words
and begged that they might meet
But Joan she loved her husband most
from his head down to his feet

She took the note to Thomas
and he began to moan
He dressed in his full armour
for Joan was his and his alone

With his faithful squire by his side
and a belly full of hate
Sir Thomas went in search of John
who was waiting by a gate

With armoured fist he hit John hard
three times upon the head
So strong the blows that Thomas dealt
soon John was very dead.

The old Knight's squire took hold of him
and told him he must flee
The faithful squire would deal with John
he would hide him where none could see

The squire lifted John up high
he threw him over the cathedral wall

'And when the dead man's found,' thought he
'they'll think he's had a fall'

But Friar John did not fall true
instead he fell sat down
And all his bumps and bruises
were hidden by his gown

Inside the cathedral walls
another friar walked nearby
His name was Brother Richard
and he began to sigh

For seeing John sat by the wall
and thinking him asleep
He threw a rock at John's bare head
but then began to weep

For Friar John slumped over
and it was clear that he was maimed
So Richard began to wail and moan
thinking he'd be blamed

Friar Richard lifted John up high
and threw him back across the wall
'And when the dead man's found,' thought he
'they'll think he's had a fall'

But Richard still felt guilty
and worried he would pay
He stole a horse tied up close by
and then he ran away

But Thomas's squire was passing by
and saw dead John slumped there
He feared the friar was haunting him
It gave him quite a scare

The squire bent down beside him
and placed a helmet on this head
So that no one else about that day
would see that John was dead

The squire lifted John up high
and tied him to his horse

He whipped the beast upon its back
with a huge amount of force

So hard the blow upon its side
the horse began to race
With dead John bouncing on its back
the helmet covering his face

It galloped hard upon the track
that Richard also took
And hearing hooves behind him
the friar turned to look

He screamed with terror loudly
at such a terrible sight
For it was the ghost of Friar John
dead eyes shining bright (in the moonlight!)

The helmet only made it worse
made John scary to behold
So Richard screamed louder still
and his blood, it ran stone cold

John had come to get him
or so foolish Richard thought
And now he begged forgiveness
for Richard had been caught

His screams were heard by others
and his arms were tied with rope
Poor Richard, he was put on trial
poor Richard had no hope

He confessed to John's foul murder
that he had thrown the stone
That he had tossed it oh so hard
it had broken flesh and bone

And so poor foolish Richard
was to hang from a nearby tree.
His execution would take place
when the clock struck three

The church bells rang out loudly
one and two and three

But up jumped old Sir Thomas
standing tall for all to see

The old knight did confess his crime
and this it was he said …
'It was I Sir Thomas Erpingham
who killed the friar dead'

Then he told one and all
of the foul friar and his fair wife
Of how the friar's love for Joan
had cost bad John his life

It seems that all agreed with him
that John had done the wrong
And so it was the knight went free
and so there ends my song*

* It's really a poem and not a song, but poem doesn't
rhyme with 'wrong' like what song does.

Of the Merry Master and his Wayward Wicked Tongue

More than 300 years ago in Norwich there lived a man called Wigget. He was the Mayor's fool and one evening he went to a banquet with all the important people of the city. At the end of the feast, everyone got up in turn and made a fine speech, but then up jumped Wigget and let out a long, loud fart! Wigget was much like John Skelton, whose tale is set down below, for he too was famous for being bad. Skelton had taught Henry VIII when the king was still a boy and he was also a priest and a poet, too. But Skelton got up to no good and was kicked out of the royal court for a while. He became rector of St Mary's Church in the small town of Diss in Norfolk, where he did even more wrong. For as the parish priest he was not meant to marry, but still he lived with a woman and she had his child.

John Skelton was a real man and the events of which I've just told are also true, but like other real people who feature in folk tales in this book, other made-up stories were drawn to him. These were comic tales that came from Germany, where the same stories were told in earlier times about another priest known as the Parson of Kellenbrough …

Long ago, young'uns, rich men were called gentlemen, even when they were not that gentle, or nice. Merry Master Skelton was such a man and most people called him a rascal, rapscallion and rogue. For although he was a man of God, Skelton was a selfish sort; a shameful show-off who was disliked by most people he met. And once when he was travelling from somewhere near to another place far away, he stopped at an inn to fill his belly full of food and sleep. Skelton feasted that evening on salted pork and bread, for this was a time when meat was rubbed with salt to stop it going bad. But so salty was the pork that John felt thirsty in the night and in need of some ale to sooth his throbbing throat. He called to the innkeeper's servant to bring him some drink, but the servant was sound asleep. Skelton called out louder still, to the innkeeper and his wife, but they were also sound asleep. Both were dreaming of the day when they would be gentlefolk and others would wait upon them.

Now perhaps, young'uns, you're wondering why Master Skelton did not get himself a drink to quickly quench his thirst. But he thought himself a gentleman, and gentlefolk do not look after themselves. 'And besides,' thought Skelton, 'besides,' thought he, 'since the innkeeper and his servants will not look after me, then I shall have some fun with them!'

And so it was, Skelton yelled out at the top of his voice, 'FIRE, FIRE, FIRE!' he called, 'FIRE, FIRE, FIRE!' called he. So loud and lusty were the merry man's calls that everyone in the inn awoke and all began to scream. The innkeeper, his wife and all their servants ran thither and yon, which meant here and there and everywhere long ago. The other guests at the inn also ran amok, bumping into benches, tripping over tables and careering over carpets, while curtains and candles came crashing down. All was hustle and bustle as the innkeeper and his wife ran from room to room, seeking out the fire in the hope that they could put it out. Meanwhile Skelton still yelled out loudly, 'FIRE, FIRE, FIRE!' as the innkeeper, his wife and all their many guests burst into his room. All of them were half-dressed and only half-awake. 'Where?' asked the innkeeper, 'where, where, where is the fire?' asked he. And John laughed at one and all in their grubby gowns and torn tunics with their knobbly knees, naked for all to see. He pointed to his mouth and yelled at the top of his voice, 'HERE, HERE, HERE!' he called. 'HERE, HERE, HERE!' called he. And merry Master Skelton demanded that the innkeeper fetch him some drink so that he might quench the flames in his mouth! Well, young'uns, there my tale ends, except to say this:

Skelton was no gentleman
but no one is all bad
I hope his tale made you laugh
and stopped you being sad

3

That craze me suffun savidge

'That craze me suffun savidge' is Norfolk dialect for 'that makes me very angry'. I've used it as the title for this chapter about wicked witchcraft and devilish doings, because the three stories below are full of anger and hate.

Of the Two Hearts Hardened by Hate

In 1531, a young woman was boiled to death on the Tuesday marketplace in King's Lynn for poisoning her mistress. Why she did it we do not know. Perhaps her mistress was cruel to her, or perhaps the servant was after her mistress's money. Either way, it was still a horrible way to punish the young woman for her crime.

But it wasn't all bad long ago, as there was also tenderness and love. Just after the Norman Conquest, a wooden castle was built in Norwich and its first constable was called Ralph Guader. He was a quarrelsome man who rebelled against King William the Conqueror, but his rebellion failed and he fled to Denmark, for the Danes were enemies of the Normans. Ralph's wife, Emma, was left in charge and held Norwich castle against King William's army for more than three months while she waited for her husband and a Danish army to come and save her, but they never came. She surrendered the castle and was sent to Brittany in France, where Ralph came to join her and where they lived the rest of their lives. Ralph was a traitor to his king, so why Emma held the castle for him is not known, although I like to

89

think that she did it because they were in love! Eventually the castle in Norwich was rebuilt in stone, which brings me neatly to two more folk tales – stories that tell of stone, love, cruelty and hate …

Norfolk has its fair share of oddities, young'uns, including two hardened hearts. The first is carved into a brick that is built into a house overlooking the Tuesday marketplace in King's Lynn, while the other is carved in stone and held in the hands of a stone-carved knight. He lies close to a stone-carved lady, in the church of Wickhampton, on the opposite side of Norfolk to King's Lynn. And so to the tales of how these two hearts became hardened by hate.

The heart of brick in King's Lynn is said to have belonged to Margaret Read, although the people called her Shady Meg. She was accused of witchcraft and burnt at the stake on the market, although in truth, young'uns, women and men accused of witchcraft were hanged for their crimes long ago. But stories grow in the telling and we should not let fact get in the way of a good story – the tale of Shady Meg did keep on growing, as did the flames that licked about her body. So fearsome was the fire that there was a loud bang and Meg's heart burst from her chest and flew like an arrow shot from a bow, splattering against the nearby brick wall. Then a spider cast a web on the spot where Meg's heart hit hard and when at last the web was blown away, there was the brick heart that can still be seen today. A gruesome tale I think you'll agree, although in a sillier version of the story, Meg's heart burst out of her body, but then bounce, bounce, bounced all the way to the nearby river, where it leapt in and swam away. And so, young'uns, if the first version of this tale is too horrible for you, then take the second, for it's both foul and fun at the same time!

But now we must talk of love for a short while, which is just as foul to some of you I'm sure! For now we travel to the church in Wickhampton where the other of our two hardened hearts does lie. Some say the stone-carved knight is Sir William Gerbygge and that he clasps his heart in his hands to show his love for his lady who lies close by. Others

say that Sir William was carved holding a stone heart to show his love for God, for he lived well over 700 years ago and the English were more religious back then. But where there is love, there is also hate and another more hateful tale to explain Sir William's hard stone heart.

For once, long ago, there were two brothers whose family owned the land where the village of Wickhampton and its church still stand to this day. Know that there is another tale of two brothers in this book – both poor, but good men who worked together to try and pull a chest full of treasure from a perilous pit. But the brothers in this story were very different indeed, for they were the sons of a rich man who had just died and both brothers always wanted what the other had. The eldest, Gilbert, argued that he should have more of their dead father's land, because he was the firstborn son. But the youngest brother, William, said that it should be him who got more land, because their father had loved him best.

Well, what started as an argument soon became a fight using fists. Red-faced and roaring, each brother beat the other, tearing at flesh and breaking bone. They fought all day and looked more like wild wolves than men. The poor people who lived nearby were too scared to stop them and so they continued brawling into the night. Their fierce fight continued until both brothers thrust their hands into the other's chest and pulled out each other's hearts! Each brother killed the other stone dead, for it was said that God was so angered by their fight that he turned the two brothers' dead bodies to stone. Only then did the poor people carry William's body to the church in Wickhampton and Gilbert's to the church in Halvergate, a village nearby. Although in those days they say that the villages were called Wicked Hampton and Hell Fire Gate, because of the two brothers' brutal ways.

The stories of two hearts hardened by hate are ended, but think on, young'uns. For some say that Shady Meg was a wicked woman, who was hated by her neighbours in King's Lynn. But I think she was innocent of her crimes and that the brothers of Wickhampton were much more wicked still. Their hearts were as cold in life as ever they were when carved in stone.

Of the Boastful Big-Head and the Devilish Difficult Deed

Norfolk was once famous for the weaving of woollen cloth, and in Tudor times sheep were farmed all over the county. Land was fenced off to keep sheep in and the poor people who once farmed that land were forced to find work in towns and cities like Norwich. They were called vagrants and often whipped from the places where they went to seek work. So many poorer people in Norfolk hated the rich sheep farmers who had taken their land, and it led to rebellions like Kett's, also mentioned in this book.

But later on things changed, because of men like Sir Thomas Coke. He was a gentleman farmer born more than 250 years ago and was famous for improving Norfolk's farmland so that crops grew taller and stronger. Coke also lowered the rents for poor farmers, to encourage them back to the land. And so to a tale about another Norfolk farmer, Berney Brograve,

although he was not a gentleman like Sir
Thomas. He lived about the same time as Coke,
but this folk tale about him is, of course, not
true – and there are other versions of boastful
Berney's story from North America, Norway
and Russia, where instead of dealing with the
Devil, a farmer makes a bargain with a bear …

NORFOLK FOLK TALES FOR CHILDREN

Of the many men and women who appear in my book, young'uns, there are few as bad as Sir Berney Brograve. Not even John Skelton, whose wearisome wit won him many enemies, was ever as bad as Brograve. Even the vicious Viking brothers, Ingvar and Ubba, were not always as cruel as Berney and his foul family. His own father killed another gentleman in a duel, while another of his family murdered a child long ago. Sir Berney himself invited the ghosts of his ferocious forebears to dinner one Old Year's Night. They were all mean men who had died dreadful deaths and that evening they celebrated their wicked ways. It's hardly surprising that the Devil would one day pay Sir Berney Brograve a visit!

And so it was that one day Brograve rode to his manor of Worstead where his men were taking too long harvesting a field of black beans and Sir Berney wanted to know why. Know that harvesting fields long ago was much harder than today. There were no tractors to help farm workers with their toil – instead they used sharp sickles and scythes, curved blades to cut their crops. It was hard, back-breaking work, made harder still because it was done in late summer when the sun shone hot. Not that Sir Berney cared as he shouted at his men, calling them all '**LAZY, SLOTHFUL SLUGGARDS AND IDLE DO-NOTHING DULLARDS, MORE LIKE STOP-A-BED CHILDREN THAN LIVELY, LUSTY YOUNG MEN!**'

Such was Sir Berney's anger that he leapt from his horse and began to scythe the field himself. 'This is how you wield a scythe,' said Sir Berney, 'this is how it's done,' said he, while he continued scolding his men for their lazy ways. 'Why I'm so good at mowing these beans,' said Berney, 'that not even the Devil himself could mow quicker than me!'

Now, young'uns, I know that many of you don't believe in the Devil, so Brograve's words won't seem foolish to you. I'm not sure that I really believe in the Devil himself, but I'm a storyteller and so cautious and careful enough to know that you should never take the Devil's name in vain. I'm not a boastful big-head like Sir Berney and know that in his story the Devil did suddenly appear. Up he popped, right beside Berney Brograve in the field of beans, and he challenged the shameful show-off to a competition to be held the following day. 'If,' said the Devil, 'if,' said he, 'you can cut more beans than me, then I shall forget your bragging words and blustering ways.' And, smiling at Brograve, the Devil waved a cloth bag in front of the old fella's face. 'But,' said the Devil, 'but,' said he, 'know, Sir Berney Brograve, that if I beat you, I'll put your soul in this old sack and hang it from a hook in the fiery furnaces of Hell for the rest of time to come – and perhaps even longer still!' Well, Sir Berney's farm servants ran and hid, and if I'd have been there I'd have hidden, too. But not

Sir Berney Brograve – instead he shook hands with the Devil as they agreed to harvest half the field each. Then the Devil disappeared as quick as he had come.

When it came to what happened next, we storytellers disagree. Some say that Berney went to a blacksmith and bought some iron rods that he planted in the Devil's side of the field. But I think that Sir Berney ordered his farm servants to pick up all the flint stone from his side of the land and scatter it where the Devil would be working the following day. For as any of you young'uns who live in Norfolk probably know, our county is covered in sharp, shiny flint. It was used for making stone tools long ago and it's as hard as any iron bar. But whether flint or iron, the outcome was the same. The following day the Devil came back and both he and Sir Berney set to cutting the bean stalks, both of them working hard. But while Sir Berney cut the stalks in his half of the field quickly, the Devil found it tough going, for his scythe kept blunting upon the sharp, shiny flint. Well, the Devil had better things to do than sharpen scythes all day and so he declared Sir Berney the winner and as I heard tell, young'uns, he went back to Hell to rest awhile, before getting up to his bad business somewhere else.

Sir Berney Brograve beat the Devil himself, but the Devil never forgot. And so it was that when Sir Berney finally dropped down dead, the Devil would not take him to Hell. Instead he was left to wander the world as a tormented spirit who would never find rest. So, young'uns, if ever you are on the road between Waxham and Worstead late at night, when the moon has taken over from the sun, maybe you'll see Sir Berney running as if Old Shuck or Jack o'Lantern is hard on his heels. And if you don't know who Old Shuck and Jack o'Lantern are, then you still have more stories to read in this book!

Of the Wicked Wyrm and the Burly, Bold Blacksmith

During the Civil War in England, fighting broke out in Norwich between the Royalists, who supported the King, and the Puritans, who all followed Oliver Cromwell and Parliament. It was the year 1648 and the Royalists broke into the Committee House where guns were kept. But a spark set fire to more than eighty barrels of gunpowder and they exploded, killing forty people. It became known as the Great Blowe, and I mention it here because all that fire and flame puts me in mind of the Ludham Wyrm, the dragon story set down below.

Most dragons come from mountainous places with great caves where they tend to sleep. But Norfolk is quite flat, so not an ideal place for dragons to live! That's not to say that Norfolk knew nothing of dragons, for they can be found in Norwich, carved in wood in Dragon Hall and in stone on the Ethelbert

Gate that leads into Norwich Cathedral. And every year long ago Norwich Snap, a man inside a dragon built of canvas, chased the children and scared them with his snapping mouth as part of the St George's Guild procession. There are also carvings of dragons in many Norfolk churches, including two serpents attacking a man in Horning church, just a few miles from Ludham where the next story is set. The tale of this wicked wyrm may have been inspired by stories told by the Vikings, who attacked and then settled in Norfolk long ago. Even today many of the street names in Norwich end in the word 'gate', which is a Danish word for a street or passage. They left their Viking words here and their stories, too, for I think that the tale below grew out of the earlier Scandinavian story of the 'Lindworm', a serpent-like dragon who, just like the Ludham Wyrm, made its home under churchyards, where it would feast upon the buried bodies of the dead …

Know all you young'uns reading this, that the small village of Ludham sits in the middle of the Norfolk Broads – the wetlands, lakes and marshes that cover the east of the county. Perhaps some of you have sailed, rowed, or even paddled upon the Broads? If you haven't, you should, especially in winter when all is quiet and the waters are silent and still, more like a mirror than a river or lake. But although my story starts in winter, all was not calm in Ludham long ago, for a wyrm, a wriggling slithering serpent, had made the village its home.

He was a ferocious, fearsome fiery dragon, who found Ludham to its liking – especially the tunnels that ran beneath the church. He wriggled and slithered inside and slept soundly while the sun shone, but each night he would creep out to steal sheep, pigs and even young'uns like you who ignored their mother's warnings about the wyrm's terrible teeth and cruel claws. He ate and he ate till he grew to more than 120ft long, which is over thirty of you young'uns laid head to toe, or even three school buses laid end to end. Now I know that some of you might not believe me, but remember, dragons, like stories, grow in the telling!

The big beast grew bigger still, while the tunnels he called home also grew beneath Ludham, as the wyrm dug and he dug with his giant claws, so that they ran under the houses, shops and pubs above. And so it was, while the great dragon snored loudly throughout the day, the houses of Ludham shuddered and shook.

Such was the noise that the people could no longer hear themselves talking in the street or singing in the church on Sundays. All were but whispers when compared with the roaring and snoring of the bellowing beast below!

The people of Ludham were scared, for they knew many a terrible tale of dreadful dragons, including one that sent terrifying tongues of fire down upon the hero Beowulf, flames that wrapped themselves around the old king like a great red cloak. They also knew of the dragon in the story of the Viking king, Ragnar Lodbrok, who ate all those who tried to save a fair maiden called Thora. You can know it too if you can find it hidden somewhere else in this book. The people of Ludham feared for their lives and also their property, for they knew that the wyrm beneath their village would eat anything or anyone that stumbled into his deep, dark and dank domain: the tunnels that the dragon called home.

Well, each and every day while the dragon was sleeping in the tunnels beneath, the people of Ludham would block up the entrance with rocks collected from the fields. But each and every night the wyrm would burst out through the stones, covering the village in dust and flame as he flew from the tunnels, red-eyed and roaring. Each night he soared up high into the sky while his hard scaly body glowed green, then blue, then red and even golden, lit by the fire that burnt deep inside his belly. He was like a fearful firework display that none did enjoy.

But then one summer's afternoon, the dragon came out of his lair early, wriggling and writhing through the long grass so as not to be seen. Now why the wyrm came out when it was still light I do not know, young'uns, but perhaps he was fed up with lying in the deep, dank earth and wished to warm himself in the late summer sun. Whatever the reason, the children of Ludham saw the beast and shouted loudly, what they called 'raising the hue and cry' long ago. They shouted a warning to all, that the wyrm was out of its tunnels and that all should beware.

Most of the villagers ran away, but there was one who did not; he was the blacksmith, a man who worked with fire, hammer and iron. He came from his forge and, like both Beowulf and Ragnar before him, he was a hero in the making. It may have been because he was a blacksmith well-used to the heat and flame of his fiery forge. It may have been his strength, from heaving a heavy hammer all day long. Whatever it was, he was not scared of the dragon. With blackened bare arms, the blacksmith lifted up a great flint rock as big as he was tall and dropped it in the entrance to the creature's cavernous caves. It was a rock so large, hard and shiny that even the mighty dragon could not shift it. Even though he blasted it with flame and lashed and thrashed at the stone with his cruel claws and terrible tail, he could not break it.

Fiery and twisted in his anger, the dangerous dragon flew up high, high, high into the sky and then swept low, low, low over the land, his wings outstretched like the sails of a Viking long ship of long ago. He flew over the Ludham marshes to St Benet's Abbey, a place where once monks had lived and prayed to God. And just as the monks who had once lived at the abbey had wished to be away from people like us, now the wily wyrm had had enough of men, women and young'uns like you. He swooped low over the abbey, so low he knocked down many of the old and ancient walls so that the abbey became the crumbling ruins you can still see today. The weary, but still scary, wyrm wriggled and writhed and slithered and slid into tunnels beneath the abbey, while the people of Ludham followed close behind. They threw the rubble, rocks and ruins of St Benet's Abbey into the great hole that the great beast had made and he was never ever seen again.

Or was he?

Now there's a question, young'uns. For if you ever find yourself upon the Norfolk Broads, sailing, rowing or even paddling past St Benet's

Abbey, then you might just see large holes in the banks of the river close by the ruins. There are some that say that the Ludham wyrm still lives, and that the holes are the many entrances to his deep, dark and dank domain. They also say that if you visit St Benet's at night when the moon casts its slight and slender shadows across the land, that sometimes a rumbling and a moaning can be heard. It might be distant thunder that warns of a coming storm, or bulls bellowing in the nearby fields; but maybe, just maybe, it's the Ludham dragon snoring as he sleeps – waiting until all is quiet in the world above so he can come a-wriggling and a-writhing and a-slithering and a-sliding and eat anything or anyone who did not hear, or heed my tale!

4

Tha's a rare ol' rummun hin'tut

'Tha's a rare ol' rummun hin'tut' is Norfolk dialect for 'that's very unusual and strange isn't it'. I've used it as the title for this chapter about ghastly and gruesome goings on because the next three stories are very strange indeed.

Of the Hellish Hound – Friend or Foe?

More than 1,000 years ago the Danish King Sweyn and his Viking warriors attacked Saxon Norwich, burning it to the ground.

It was revenge for the Saxon King Ethelred's attack on the Danes in England, where many including Sweyn's own sister had been killed. The Viking raid was a disaster for Norwich, but other towns in Norfolk have also suffered through time. In Great Yarmouth seventy-nine people died in 1845 when the Haven Suspension Bridge collapsed after hundreds of people gathered there to see a clown called Nelson float by in a barrel towed by four geese.

Both these events are included here because both involve death, doom and gloom, which fits well with many of the stories of Old Shuck, the black dog who some say is a hound from Hell and stalks the roads of Norfolk and the whole of East Anglia. Some of the tales do put Shuck near Yarmouth and he might even have a link with Vikings like King Sweyn, for Norfolk was once part of the Viking 'Danelaw' – land given to them by the Saxon king, Alfred the Great, more than 1,100 years ago, which stretched from Essex, well below Norfolk, to Yorkshire well above. And many of the places covered by Danelaw have tales of black dogs, although they go by other names in other counties. Some think that the tales of Shuck come from Viking myths and legends about Fenrir, the great wolf, or from their folk tales about shape-shifting 'Varulv', what we would call werewolves today. Others say he comes from Anglo-Saxon folklore and that his name Shuck comes from the Saxon word 'soucca', which meant 'demon'. Some Norfolk people believe him to be the faithful wolf who once guarded King Edmund's head long ago, which is another story you can find here in my book. But read this one first!

When I was as young as you, young'uns, I scared very easily. Whether it was stories of ghosts or goblins, witches or will o' wisps, it didn't take a lot to send me shivering to my bed. And the stories that scared me most of all were those about Black Shuck. I remember

once when I'd been fishing on Acle marshes one winter's evening with my friends; of how on the way home my fishing rod was snagged upon a tree and I was left alone on the track. My friends had all walked away and the stories of Black Shuck came creeping into my head. I remembered how once Black Shuck had burst into Blythburgh church, his eyes burning brightly, as thunder clapped overhead. He killed a man and a boy that night and left scorch marks on the north door. But Blythburgh is in Suffolk, far away from Norfolk where I lived, and it happened long ago.

But wait! There was another story about a man who had been fishing on Great Yarmouth beach late at night. He heard hateful howls behind him and, looking around, saw Black Shuck growling grimly, coming close to where he stood. The fisherman ran into the sea and the next day he was found shivering and shaking, up to his knees in the salt water, while his once black hair had turned white! Like many people, he believed that Shuck was a portent of doom, which meant that anyone who saw the shaggy black hound would die very soon. Remembering that tale, I was frantic to free my fishing rod, but still it was snagged fast. I thought about leaving the rod hanging there, but it was a birthday present from my parents and they would be upset, angry even, if I did not bring it home. And so it was, I tried to think of happier tales about Black Shuck, for in stories he's not always bad. There was one I'd heard where he'd saved a girl who was being followed by a very bad man. Old Shuck, with his hair as black as night and his eyes as red as fierce flames, had chased the man away. In that tale Shuck was a heroic hound, a good and faithful dog, and here is another such tale that I remembered on Acle marshes when I was but a boy.

Once, long ago, a small sailing ship called a brig was sailing around the coast of Norfolk, weighed down with fruit and spices to be sold in London, although the ship would never make port. A great storm snatched up the small brig, tossing it all ways upon the waves, and the sailors on board wept and wailed while the captain of the ship called for calm. He ordered his men to 'hold fast', while he held one hand upon the helm, the steering wheel of the brig, and the other on the collar of his dog, a huge deerhound, who was the captain's true and faithful friend.

But the storm grew worse and seeing that the
ghastly gales were breaking his ship in two, the
captain called for the crew to save themselves.
'Abandon ship,' shouted the captain, 'abandon
ship,' shouted he, as all leapt into the stinging,
stormy seas and desperately swam towards the
lights that lit the land. Lights that were so close,
yet so far away. For none made it to safety that
night. All drowned in the wicked waters off the

Norfolk coast. And in the first light of day the people of Salthouse, where the ship's timbers and crew had washed ashore, gathered up the flotsam and jetsam – the wood, ropes, sails and cargo that they would keep for themselves. They even took the rings off the dead sailors' fingers, once prayers had been said over their sad sea-soaked bodies.

The people of Salthouse continued their search until at last they found the captain's corpse lying next to his dead deerhound. The lifeless man's fingers were locked around his dog's collar, while the deerhound's jaws were still clamped to his master's coat. It was clear to all that mournful morning that both man and dog had tried to save each other. Such was the bond between the captain and his faithful hound that it was hard to free his coat from the dog's jaws, or his fingers from the animal's collar. When at last it was done, they buried the captain and his crew in Salthouse churchyard, but the dog would be buried alone. For the churchyard was no place for an animal, or so they believed, and so they buried him on Salthouse beach instead.

Well, young'uns, know that while both master and hound died that stormy night long ago, the bond between them did not. Tales were soon being told of a devilish dog haunting the highways and byways close to Salthouse and other villages nearby. 'A horrible hound from Hell,' some said, 'hatefully howling whenever a storm blew at sea.' But the older and wiser people of Salthouse knew, as you also now know, that it was no hound from Hell – only the ghost of the faithful deerhound, looking for his master and ever hopeful that he would one day hear the captain's call.

Well, young'uns, that tale took some of the fear away that dark night on Acle marshes long ago and eventually I was able to free my fishing rod and re-join my friends. I felt a little braver just because of one story where Shuck was a true and faithful hound. The black dog goes by many different names – 'Old Scarfe', 'Old Skeff' and even the 'Hateful Thing', which makes me think that there might be more than one huge hound roaming the roads of East Anglia, or at the very least many a different story, telling many a different version of the black beast and his ways. For stories grow in the telling and change depending on who tells them. As a storyteller I know that there is always a different point of view from your own. Remember that, young'uns, and it will always serve you well.

Of the Petrifying and Perilous Pits

Some of you will have heard of bad King John, whose noblemen led a revolt against him and made John sign Magna Carta, a document that was meant to restrict the king's powers. But John went back on the agreement and war broke out between him and his nobles. And it was while he was moving his army from King's Lynn across the Wash, the large estuary that separates Norfolk from Lincolnshire, that John's baggage carts sunk in the river mud and all his treasure was lost, while John died of dysentery just a few days later.

While it's true that John died in Lincolnshire in 1216, the story of his lost treasure is less certain. I mention it here because one of the next stories is also about treasure lost in a watery pit long ago. Stories of perilous pits are found in the myths and legends of many countries, from the Saxons and Vikings to the Ancient Mesopotamians – all tell of a terrible place beneath the earth where wicked people were punished for the rest of time. It's the place that we in England call Hell, and many believed long ago that pits and caves were the entrances to that world of the dead. Here, then, are three Norfolk stories of Hellish pits from long ago …

It would not be a lie, young'uns, to say that Norfolk is a marshy place, with its fair share of wetlands that we now call the Broads. Perhaps that's why it also has its fair share of pond-like pits and the terrible tales that have grown up around them. There is the Lily Pit near Gorleston, a town that sits by the sea. It's said to be haunted by a coach and four horses that plunged into the pit long ago. On wild wintery nights the wild whinnying of the horses and crack of the coachman's wicked whip can still be heard as they race toward their dismal doom.

If that's not frightened you enough, know that there is a small village called Aylmerton that also sits close by the sea and is haunted by a white wailing woman. For nearby, there are more than 2,000 shallow pits dug by people who lived and worked there before the time of the Romans, long ago. Most are lost to time, filled in with earth and covered by tree root, but it's still a place of great interest to archaeologists, the men and women who study people from long ago. The likes of you and me also go there for a walk, for it is a pretty peaceful place, away from the hustle and bustle of the town.

Or is it?

For when the sun goes down and the moon takes over, a shrill shrieking can often be heard as the woman in white rises from the pits, wringing her hands, weeping terrible tears and moaning mournfully for unfortunate folk to hear! It is no wonder that all who live nearby call them the 'Shrieking Pits'. Some say she is one of the ancient people who dug the pits long ago. Perhaps she fell or was buried by flint, her spirit trapped there, too. But others say that she is the ghost of a servant girl who lived some

200 years ago. Alas she fell in love with a man who was already married and would never be hers. And so it was, she took to walking the highways and byways at dusk, wringing her hands and wailing and weeping terrible tears that dropped into the deep, dark pits, into which she also fell – dragged in by an unseen hand, or did she perhaps jump, for that she could no longer live with her loneliness?

A sad tale either way, young'uns, if you believe in such things. I can't decide which one, if any, I believe, for perhaps there is no shrieking woman in white really, just the mist and the screeching of owls? If you are uncertain you could always visit the shrieking pits, but not alone. Go with family and friends, and if you do by chance see the woman in white, you could ask her who she is and why she haunts that place. But shout loudly, or you won't be heard over the noise of her screams!

I do think that it is worth visiting these places, although, as I said, not alone. It's always

best to go with grown-ups, for some of them are dangerous places. Once, my friend and I went to an old ruined church that was surrounded by stinging nettles as tall as a man. We were heading towards the church tower, the only bit of the old building still standing, because there was a story that the ground beneath was hollow, that there was a hidden pit below. We fought our way through nettle and over broken branch and into the old tower, where we began to jump up and down. The ground did feel hollow and when our feet hit the floor, it sounded like the beat of a great drum. Up and down we both jumped, again and again, until suddenly, both of us were gripped by fear and taken by terror. Without speaking to each other, we ran from that place and did not stop running for a mile or more, and know that we never went back! Now where exactly that church is I cannot say, but I can tell you that it was near another small village called Southwood that has its own putrid pond that locals call the Callow Pit.

And once, long ago, there lived two brothers, who knew the many tales of that deep dark pit – that it had no bottom but led straight to Hell. Others said that pirates hid their treasure there and that there was still gold sunk beneath the murky depths of Callow Pit, just waiting to be found. Well, the brothers had been raised on stories, told to them by their beloved grandmother as they sat of an evening by the fire. They went to bed each night full of tales of long-buried gold coins and diamonds, emeralds and the reddest of rubies, too. They dreamt of finding King John's treasure, lost in the Wash long ago. So, too, they dreamt of finding a pot of gold just as the pedlar of Swaffham had done. For his was the most famous of all Norfolk stories, and it too is hidden like treasure right here in my book.

The two brothers dreamt of finding hidden treasure, but their dreams were not idle fancy. They were poor and so in need of coin from wherever it came. And so, although there were rumours that the Callow Pit was haunted by a headless horseman and worse, they went there on a wild windy night in the hope that the wicked weather would keep others away. The two brothers brought ladders with them and placed them across the petrifying and perilous pit. And with long staffs made from branches broken from nearby trees, they climbed onto the ladders and fished and felt for the treasure hidden in the murky depths below. They pushed and prodded with their staffs for many an hour until at last one of them snagged on something heavy beneath. It was an iron ring fixed to a great wooden chest, full of gold, or so the brothers hoped. Both the young men heaved hard upon the staff and lifted the wooden chest onto the ladders that bowed and bent low beneath the great weight. 'We have it,' cried one of them, 'we have it,' cried he, while the other brother also joined in. 'It is ours and ours alone,' said he, 'and not even the Devil himself shall take it from us!' But no sooner had those words left the second brother's lips than the first began to shiver and shake. For from the foul fetid water came a colossal cruel claw that snatched hold of the treasure chest.

The poor brothers were terrified, but unwilling to give up the gold without a fight. They took hold of the iron ring atop the chest and would not let go. Again they pulled hard, but the ring broke and the wooden chest disappeared back into the dark, dismal depths from whence it came. The boys returned home with only the iron ring as proof of their tale – that they had wrestled with the Devil himself.

Some of the people of Southwood believed them and some did not. But know, young'uns, if you are one of those who doubt their tale, then after you and your family have visited the Shrieking Pits at Aylmerton, go to the church at Limpenhoe, close to Southwood. For the iron ring from the Devil's treasure chest still hangs from the church door to this day!

Of the Two Babes Wandering in the Wailing Woods

In 1751, a strange man was found wandering the streets of Norwich. His hair and beard were tangled with twigs and leaves and he could only hum and whinny like a horse. He was shut in the Bridewell, where those without work were sometimes put long ago, and in time he was identified as Peter the Wild Boy, who had been found wandering the woods as a child near Hanover, which is now part of

Germany. The men who found him there said that he ran naked on all fours and fed upon raw squirrel and crow. He was brought to England to meet the king and eventually sent to live on a farm in Hertfordshire. There he stayed for many years until one evening he disappeared, only to turn up in Norwich. His was a sad story, for he never learnt a language and could not tell of how he was lost as a child long ago. But he was well looked after in England, even in the Bridewell, where he was saved when fire burnt it down.

Peter was lucky, for children were not always so well treated long ago. In 1708, Michael Hammond, aged seven and his sister, Ann, aged eleven, were both hanged in King's Lynn in Norfolk for stealing just one loaf of bread – a cruel act that brings me to my next tale about two children also cruelly treated like Michael and Ann and lost in the woods like Peter the Wild Boy. It's a tale that's been in Norfolk for more than 400 years, but still makes me think of two German stories – *Snow White* and *Hansel and Gretel* – where children were also cruelly treated and abandoned in the woods. So as you read the next story, remember that just as Peter travelled to Norfolk from Germany long ago, part of this next folk tale may have also made the same journey much earlier still …

There are many odd-sounding names in Norfolk, young'uns, but none as strange as the 'Wailing Woods' near Watton. The real name of the woods is Wayland, although when you hear the tale I'm about to tell, you'll know why the locals still call it the Wailing Place to this day.

For once there was a family called the Trueloves: a father, mother and two children, Edgar and Jane, and all was well in their world – for a while at least. Truelove was their name and also their nature, for the father and mother loved their children dearly and both Edgar and Jane loved their parents back. But they lived long ago when people knew disease and death more than we do today, and both the mother and father fell ill. They went to the local wise woman, who was skilled in making medicines from roots and herbs, but even she could not cure the Trueloves of what ailed them and they knew in their hearts that they would die.

And so it was, Edgar and Jane's father took them to their uncle, asking that he would care for the children when he was dead and gone. He left money with the man to pay for the children's care and the uncle agreed just in time; Edgar and Jane's parents both died, leaving the two children to weep woeful tears. For never again would they know kindness; never again would they know the joy of a warm embrace. Their uncle was also a Truelove, but he loved coin even more than his own two sons and certainly more than Edgar and Jane. He wanted the children's money for his own, but it would only be his if they were dead!

The uncle was a gentleman and gentlefolk like him do not do their own dirty work. They have servants to do their bidding, be it fair or foul, and this would be foul work indeed. The unloving uncle ordered two of his men to take the children deep into Wayland Woods and kill them dead, before burying their bodies deep, so no one would know of the dark and dastardly deed. He picked two servants, well-suited to the task; Rawbones and Woldkill were their names and both were men of foul fame who had committed many a cruel crime.

They led Edgar and Jane into the woods, whistling as they walked, while the two small

children hopped over broken bough and branch, laughing and shouting, both delighted at being outside and away from their uncaring uncle. Such was the children's joy, that it moved one of the servant's hearts. Which one I know not, but he refused to kill the two innocent children and so he and the other servant did fight. Fists were thrown, daggers drawn and the kinder of the two servants killed the other dead. 'Fear not, children,' said the servant to the terrified twins, 'fear not,' said he, and he told Edgar and Jane that he would save them, although in truth he had no plan. He could not take them back to their uncle, nor could he take them home, for he was a poor man who could not afford two more mouths to feed. And so it was, the servant took them deep, deep, deeper into the woods and there left the children all alone, hoping another would find both brother and sister and take care of them as their own. But no one else came and the two children were left to starve. They ate berries and nuts and cared for each other as best they could, but winter came and wrapped herself about them as they slept beneath an old oak tree. Both Edgar and Jane died peacefully in their sleep, cheek to cheek and with their arms entwined. Then a robin redbreast covered their bodies with a blanket of leaves, while the other birds sang sorrowful songs, to mourn the loss of two such loving young'uns that day.

Two children died in the Wailing Woods as it became known, because of their uncle's wicked ways. But the truth always comes out in time and the children's money did their uncle no good. He bet and gambled the money away and his crops failed in the fields. His barn burnt down and his two grown-up sons were both drowned at sea. The unloving uncle was a Truelove by name, but not by nature. He wanted it all, but in the end the unloving uncle lost everything that he had.

And so, young'uns, if ever you visit the Wailing Woods near Watton, go in summer, for

139

it is in truth a beautiful place when the sunlight dapples the mossy earth beneath, while the birds sing brightly in the branches above. And don't dwell upon this terrible tale. Instead use your time in that beautiful place to remember all that you have and all who are dear to you.

5

Knock a blairze on mawther

'Knock a blairze on mawther' is Norfolk dialect for 'Light the fire, girl'. I've used it as the title for this chapter about the fay – the fairy folk – because the first and third story involve fire, or the wood used for making it, while the second takes place in February, when a warming fire is always welcome. The third story also includes two 'mawthers': two girls called Mary and Betty.

Of the Flinger of Flames

People in medieval times heated their houses and cooked their food upon fires made of peat – the bits of trees, grasses and other vegetation that rots beneath our feet. And in Norfolk from 600 to 900 years ago they dug up so much of it that the holes left behind flooded, forming the Broads, the shallow lakes and marshlands that cover much of the east side of Norfolk to this day. But wetlands are dangerous places and stories grew up around the Broads: tales of strange creatures that would attack lost travellers, tales of flame-flinging Jack o'Lanterns and their cousins, the Hikey Sprites, who were used as warnings to children to keep to the path.

The name Hikey Sprite may come from the Norfolk words 'high sprite', which meant a goblin or a ghost. But it might also have come from the Danish word 'hytte', which meant 'to take care'. And since the stories of Hikey Sprites and Jack o'Lanterns were used as warnings long ago, this sounds right to me. And remember that the Danish Vikings once had their stronghold in the east of Norfolk at a place called the Isle of Flegg. If you ever travel that way you'll see that many of the village names end in 'by', which was a Viking word for a small settlement long ago. So once again we see that tales from Norfolk may have started in the Viking lands of Denmark, Norway and Sweden. Even today Scandinavian people talk of the 'Lyktgubbe', meaning the Lantern Man who lures travellers to their doom with strange lights. He is one of the 'Vaesen', meaning sprites, fairies and gnomes, who are known for being very unpredictable – you never know if they will be good, or very bad, which bring us to the next tale below …

Here's a question for you young'uns – have you ever put something down that is precious to you, only to find that when you turn back it has suddenly gone? It disappeared only to reappear days, or even weeks, later? I have, and there are some that say it was the Hikey Sprite who stole from you. It was the Hikey Sprite who was playing a trick! Of Hikey Sprites, I can say little more – for now that we live in bright warm houses with indoor bathrooms, central heating and electric lights, it is unlikely that we will ever see one. Nowadays we stay

inside in the twilight times, watching telly and playing games online, but just imagine a time when young'uns like you still played out after dark. I did when I was a boy long ago. And just imagine a time even further back when my mum, Mary, was a girl. She too lives on among the pages of this book and if you've read her tale already, you'll know that she had to use an outside toilet at the bottom of the garden whenever nature called.

Imagine being a small child like Mary, creeping up that path in the dead of night with only a candle to light your way to the loo, fearful that the Hikey Sprite would leap out from the bushes and get you! People knew when the Hikey Sprite was lurking nearby on a cold winter's night long ago, because the dog would growl and bark loudly and the cat would refuse to go out! But others said that the Hikey Sprite was a good imp, a guardian fairy, who would watch over young'uns like you, making sure that you didn't fall through the ice of a frozen pond, or set fire to your bedroom by leaving the candle burning all night. Like most imps, elves and fairies, the Hikey had two sides. He could be good and kind if he wanted, or mischievous and even very evil if he was annoyed!

I only mention the Hikey Sprite here because he was similar to other sprites wandering the highways, byways, trackways and pathways of Norfolk long ago. What some said was marsh gas burning brightly far away, others claimed was Jack o' Lanterns dancing on the marshes and getting up to no good. Sometimes known as the Will o'Wisps, Lantern Men, or even Jenny Burnt Arses in times past, they were tiny terrible creatures for, unlike Hikey Sprites, they were always very bad! On cold cruel nights they held flickering flames high above their heads to lure terrified travellers to their dire doom, into the marrow-chilling marshy wastes, never to be heard of again. On 'roky' nights, which is what Norfolk people called misty evenings long ago, Jack o'Lanterns ran after anyone who used a lamp to light their way. They would smash the terrified traveller's light to pieces, leaving them in the dark, or even chase them all the way home. Near a small village called Irstead, in Norfolk, Jack o'Lanterns were said to be at their worst, although some of the people from Irstead thought that there was only one Jack o'Lantern and that he was the ghost of a murderous man who had been drowned for his cruel crimes. 'Neatishead Jack' some called him, named after a village nearby. And once there was a farmer on the edge of the village who didn't believe in Jack o'Lanterns at all, but one night one of the tiny terrible creatures followed him home from a fair and set fire to his curtains. The frightened farmer hadn't believed in Jack o'Lanterns before that night, but he did after that!

Now whether or not you believe in Jack o'Lanterns, young'uns, whether you believe them ghosts, imps, or perhaps just flickering marsh gas, know that if ever you meet one of their kind upon the road, you should do as the wiser people of Irstead did long ago – throw yourself flat upon the track and hold your breath until Jack has gone back to the marrow-chilling marshy mires that he calls home.

Of the Giver of Gifts

In 1600, a man called Will Kemp ended his 'nine dais wonder' in Norwich. He had danced all the way from London to Norfolk's capital city in just nine days, with the bells round his ankles jingling as he finished his jig by leaping over the wall surrounding St John's churchyard.

Will Kemp was a colourful comic actor who gave gifts of garters to all those who danced with him, brightly coloured bands that were tied round your legs long ago. And that's why I've mentioned him here in the introduction to the tale of Jack Valentine. For Jack was a comic character like Will Kemp and also a giver of gifts. And like many of the Scandinavian sprites mentioned in the introduction to the first story in this chapter, he could be both naughty and nice ...

Know, young'uns, that while some of the stories collected here in my book are very like stories from other lands, the tale of Jack Valentine seems to have started right here in Norfolk. He is a custom, a bit of folklore that has been passed down through individual families, so not everyone in Norfolk knew about him long ago and even in Norwich today not everyone has heard tell of Jack Valentine, the giver of gifts. But as people have moved from Norfolk and even England too, they have taken the tradition with them. I have heard tell that there are some people who now get gifts from Jack Valentine in Australia! Folklore, traditions and customs travel from one land to another and, just like stories, they grow in the telling. This was certainly true of Jack Valentine, because he is also known as Mother Valentine, Father Valentine, or even Snatch, but more of that below.

When I was a child like you, I never gave much thought to who or what Jack Valentine was. The presents he left were more important to me. For Jack always left gifts on the front doorstep on the evening of St Valentine's Day. We think of St Valentine's as a day of romance, for sending cards to your boyfriend or girlfriend and even chocolates and flowers, too. It was slushy and soppy like that long ago, but it was also a time for young'uns like you – as soon as it grew dark Jack Valentine would knock loudly upon the front door and when it was opened there would be the gift wrapped in newspaper waiting to be unwrapped. Perhaps sweets, crayons, plasticine, or even a spud-gun if Jack Valentine was feeling generous!

But Jack was an imp like the Hikey Sprite who also gets a mention in this chapter. And, like the Hikey, he could be mischievous when the mood took him. That's why some people call him Snatch Valentine, because when children went to pick up their newspaper-wrapped packages, Jack would pull them quickly away with a piece of string. The young'uns would have to chase their presents down the garden path, although they always caught them when Jack Valentine had had his fun!

It wasn't until I was older that I realised that it was not Jack, but my dad, who brought the gifts, with the help of neighbours and friends. He would go out on the evening of St Valentine's Day, saying he was taking the dog for a walk. But instead he was leaving presents for our neighbour's children on their doorstep. It was he who knocked loudly on their front door before running quickly away. There was a deal to be done, you see, between my father and our neighbour, for then he would go out, pretending to his own children that he had a job to do, although our neighbour couldn't say that he was going to walk the dog as my dad did, for he didn't have a dog and you can't really walk the cat! Whatever his excuse, our neighbour would leave gifts upon our front doorstep, before he too knocked loudly and quickly ran away.

Well, young'uns, I feel a bit guilty, giving the game away and telling you all that Jack Valentine is not real. But take no notice of me, for Jack will always be with us as long as we keep the tradition going and as long as we keep the folklore alive. I did my bit when my children, Joe and Sam, were young. They always got a gift from the generous imp as darkness fell on St Valentine's Day. Not that it was always easy because we have lived in faraway places, with no neighbours nearby to help with the fun and games. Once we lived on a houseboat on the edge of South Walsham Broad, not far from Irstead, where Jack o'Lantern gets up to no good, and having no neighbours nearby to leave my children's presents, I would have to leave them myself. I told my children that I was going out for some reason, that there was an important job I needed to do. I waited a few minutes, then left their gifts upon the bank and beat three times hard upon the houseboat door. Then quickly I ran to hide, but it was dark and I could not see the way. And so it was, I crouched low behind a twisted tree, forgetting that there was an old pond there full of mud and weed. An old pond into which I stepped, filling my boots with icy water and stinking sticky sludge!

Now the reason that I told you all of my welly full of mud, young'uns, is this: maybe I should have taken more care, I should have thought about where I was going to hide. But then again, it was perhaps not my fault. Maybe, just maybe, it was mischievous Jack Valentine who pushed me into the pond. Maybe, just maybe, Jack was getting his own back on me, because I no longer believed!

Of the Collector of Coins

In Tudor times, Norfolk and its capital city Norwich were famous for hand weaving woollen cloth like worsted, which was named after one of the villages where it was made. Dutch and Flemish weavers came here more than 400 years ago and helped make our cloth finer and more famous still. But then came the Industrial Revolution when factories full of machines took over from hand weaving and most of them were built in the north of England. So the people of Norfolk had to find other ways to make money, and in Norwich that meant making shoes. Norwich became famous for its large shoe factories and people came from other parts of England to work in them. Some of my own mother's family came to Norfolk more than 100 years ago to do just that.

Her family were called the Fishers and this is a tale of just two of them, my mum Mary and her sister, Betty. I've included it in this chapter about fairy folk because Betty was much like the naughty Hikey Sprites and Jack Valentine, who also appear in this chapter. She could be very kind just as fairies so often are, always giving us children sweets and cakes, yet my mum said that Betty could be selfish and naughty like an imp whenever the mood took her. She was also a trickster, what some called a scallywag in times past, well-suited to this tale. For although the story below belongs only to Mary and Betty, trickster tales can be found throughout the world; from Anansi the spider in West African legends to Reynard the fox in French folklore. And like all tricksters, Betty the collector of coin played upon the greed, pride and foolishness of others, and she and my mum had many adventures in Norwich, of which this is just one ...

For me, young'uns, folk tales are simply the stories that are passed down from one generation to another. And some of them include real people like Master John Skelton and Sir Thomas Erpingham, who both behave badly within the pages of this book. Real people can and do pop up in folk tales, including my mum, Mary and her sister, Betty. They were both born long ago, between the First and Second World Wars, and just like characters in many a folk tale, they had a hard life. They grew up in a small terraced house, for there were long lines of them in Norwich, built in raggedy rows, each one leaning upon the next one along. Many people still live in terraced houses today, although they are much nicer than they used to be. No longer do the people who live in them have to go outside to the toilet or wash themselves in a tin bath in front of the fire. Imagine that! My mum said that the terraced houses were like plants that grew in a row, for each of them could hold a large family crammed in tight like sardines, or flowers in a flowerbed. Mary and Betty were two of twelve children, who along with their parents shared one small terraced house. It was so small there was not room to swing a cat and there were cracks in the walls where Mother Winter's wicked wind found its way through. The twelve children were 'topped and tailed' in their beds, sleeping four or more to one mattress, each with their feet poking out next to their sleeping brother or sister's nose. Imagine that! To make matters worse, they only had old coats and newspapers to cover them while they slept, for blankets they had none.

Their father would mend their shoes by reheeling them with old bike tyres, and other children would mock and laugh at Mary and Betty. For just as children can be cruel today, so too they could be nasty long ago. Mary would go with her mother to Norwich market late on a Saturday afternoon when all the market stalls were about to close in the hope they would pick up a cheap scrag-end of meat. And Mary's father and brothers always got to eat their fill first, for some thought boys more important than girls long ago. Mary even had to mend her brothers' manky socks. Imagine that! And each and every night Mary's mother would take out her small purse with seven leather pockets in it and move her few pennies from one pocket to another, trying to make what little coin they had last the week. They called it 'robbing Peter to pay Paul' long ago.

Mary and Betty had hard lives, but still they looked forward to each new day and loved Saturdays best of all. Their brothers enjoyed 'bullock-whopping' on a Saturday afternoon – helping the cattlemen drive cows and bulls through the streets to the cattle market that was still held in the middle of Norwich long ago. Each of the brothers had his own bullock-whopping stick which, when not being used all, sat on the mantelpiece, over the fire, taking pride of place. But Mary and Betty had no whopping sticks, for the boys did not let the girls join in. But they didn't mind, for they were more interested in the cinema; going to the pictures is what Mary and Betty loved most. But the cinema cost coin and they had none. Sometimes Mary's older brother, Peter, would help, for he always had some money. He would buy them gobstoppers as a treat, although they had to suck and suck them quickly before they got home so that their mother did not know that Peter had wasted money upon sweets. He would make them spit out their gobstoppers into the river before they got home, although Mary would hide hers in her knickers and pretend she had finished it. She would take it out later to suck and suck some more, but by now the sticky gobstopper was covered in knicker fluff and so was not that sweet at all!

But one Saturday Peter was not about and so Mary went in search of Betty, for she always found a way of making some money, turning one coin into two. First Betty and Mary gathered up what rags they could find to sell to the rag and bone man. He bought them to be recycled into paper and carpets, for nothing was wasted long ago. With the few pennies they made selling rags, Betty and Mary brought some bundles of kindling, thin sticks used to help start a fire, for a penny each.

Then the two girls bet their brothers that they could not split each stick in two with their father's axe. 'You're just silly boys, you

are,' said Betty and Mary, 'you're just rubbish boys,' said they, as, poking out their tongues at their brothers, Betty and Mary mocked them some more. 'If you try and chop them sticks, you're sure to chop your fingers off instead,' said Betty as she winked at Mary, and both shared a laugh. And with good reason, for the two girls knew that their brothers, just like all boys, just like Tom Hickathrift, whose story starts this book, liked to show off. Of that I'm sure all the girls reading this will agree! For Betty and Mary's older brothers stole their father's axe and each took turns carefully chopping the thin sticks thinner still, while trying to keep all their fingers and thumbs! And all the time that they were chopping, Betty and Mary pretended to be impressed, saying, 'oooh' and 'aaah' and 'wow'. Eventually their brothers finished and were well pleased with their work. Happy that they had shown the two girls how brilliant boys could be, they left to fetch their bullock-whopping sticks, while Betty and Mary laughed long, loud and lustily at their brothers' foolish ways. For they gathered up the sticks and tied them as before, but they had doubled their bundles – they had many, many more! I wrote a rhyme there by accident young'uns, and I liked it so much that I'm going to finish this tale with another:

> Having doubled their bundles, they sold them on
> and so doubled their coin that day
> Off to the pictures, the two sisters went
> with plenty of pennies to pay

Well, young'uns, there my Norfolk folk tales do come to an end, and all that is left for me to say is goodbye. Or, as we say here in Norfolk, 'fare thee well together'.

Glossary

Alas - a pity
Ale - a drink like beer
Amok - out of control
Axle - the shaft between two wheels
Besieged - surrounded by an enemy
Braggart - a boastful person
Brawling - fighting
Brutally - very violently
Clouted Shoon - boots with nails in the soles
Constable - the person in charge of a castle
Court - a ruler's meeting place
Dullard - a stupid person
Dysentery - very bad diarrhoea
Estuary - where a river meets the sea
Forebears - family from the past
Friar - a member of a religious group

Guild - a group of people who look after each other

Heed - to pay attention

Lethargic - tired

Maimed - seriously injured

Manor - land controlled by a lord

Marrow - fatty stuff in your bones

Measly - small

Mettlesome - brave

Mires - marshy ground

Monk - a member of a religious group

Mourn - sadness at someone's death

Pious - deeply religious

Plunder - steal

Quench - to satisfy thirst

Scolding - arguing loudly

Scrag-end - boney and thin

Sheaf - a small bundle of straw

Slothful - lazy

Sluggard - a lazy person

Sovereign - the ruler of a country

Squire - servant to a Lord

Toil - hard work

Union - like a guild, a group of people who look after each other

Vagabonds - a person without a job or home

Woeful - very sad

Bibliography

Briggs, K., *British Folk Tales and Legends – A Sampler* (Granada, 1977) (Routledge & Kegan Paul, 1970).

Crossley-Holland, K., *British Folk Tales – New Versions* (Orchard Books, 1987).

Dixon, G.M., *Folktales and Legends of Norfolk* (Minimax Books, 1987).

Duggan, A., & Haase, D., *Folktales and Fairy Tales: Traditions and Texts from Around the World* (Greenwood, 2016).

Egerkrans, J., *Vaesen – Spirits and Monsters of Scandinavian Folklore* (2017).

Glyde, J. Jun., *Folklore and Customs of Norfolk* (EP Publishing Ltd, 1973).

Hartland, E.S., *English Fairy and Other Folk Tales* (The Walter Scott Publishing Company, 1890).

Haymon, S., *Norwich* (Longman Young Books, 1973).

Heaton, T., *Nasty Norwich* (Bosworth Books, 2005).

Howet, P., *Norfolk Ghosts and Legends* (Countryside Books, 1993).

Howet, P., *Tales of Old Norfolk* (Countryside Books, 1991).

Jewson, C.B., *People of Medieval Norwich* (Jarrolds, 1928).

Kerven, R., *English Fairy Tales and Legends* (National Trust Books, 2008).

Loveday, R., *Hikey Sprites – The Twilight of a Norfolk Tradition* (Swallowtail Print Ltd, 2009).

Lupton, H., *Norfolk Folk Tales* (The History Press, 2013).

Marshall, S., *Everyman's Book of English Folktales* (J.M. Dent & Sons, 1981).

Maskill, L., *Norfolk Dialect* (Bradwell Book, 2013).

Philip, N., *The Penguin Book of English Folktales* (Penguin Books, 1991).

Shah, I., *World Tales* (Penguin Books, 1979).

Schram, P., *Jewish Stories One Generation Tells Another* (Rowman and Littlefield Publishers, 2005).

Storey, N.R., *The Little Book of Norfolk* (The History Press, 2011).

Tong, C.M., Like Plants We Grow in a Row, *The Eastern Daily Press* (1972–76).

Websites and Links

Hidden East Anglia, hiddenea.com

Norfolk dialect and people, www.literarynorfolk.co.uk

Similar tales to the Pedlar of Swaffham, www. pitt.edu/~dash/type1645.html

Some Norfolk myths and legends, http:// myths.e2bn.org/mythsandlegends

Weird Norfolk, www.edp24.co.uk/topic/Tag/ Weird%20Norfolk

Society *for* **Storytelling**

Since 1993, the Society for Storytelling has championed the art of oral storytelling and the benefits it can provide – such as improving memory more than rote learning, promoting healing by stimulating the release of neuropeptides, or simply great entertainment! Storytellers, enthusiasts and academics support and are supported by this registered charity to ensure the art is nurtured and developed throughout the UK.

Many activities of the Society are available to all, such as locating storytellers on the Society website, taking part in our annual National Storytelling Week at the start of every February, purchasing our quarterly magazine *Storylines*, or attending our Annual Gathering – a chance to revel in engaging performances, inspiring workshops, and the company of like-minded people.

You can also become a member of the Society to support the work we do. In return, you receive free access to *Storylines*, discounted tickets to the Annual Gathering and other storytelling events, the opportunity to join our mentorship scheme for new storytellers, and more. Among our great deals for members is a 30% discount off titles in the *Folk Tales* series from The History Press website.

For more information, including how to join, please visit

www.sfs.org.uk

If you liked *Norfolk Folk Tales for Children*...

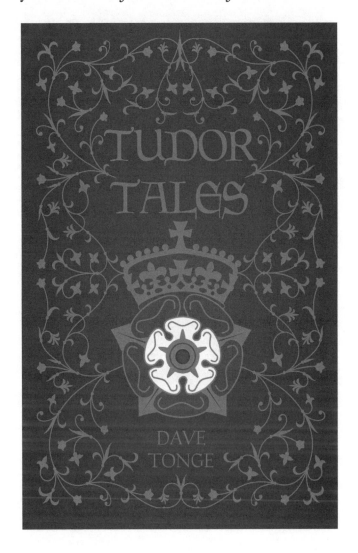

THE NORFOLK STORY BOOK

WRITTEN BY **ISABELLE KING**

ILLUSTRATED BY
JOHN McKEEVER

CHIP COLQUHOUN

CAMBRIDGESHIRE

FOLK TALES FOR CHILDREN

Oceans Of
PRAYER

PRAYER Oceans Of

Compiled by

Maureen Edwards and Jan S Pickard

Cover photo and graphics: Mark Howard

A co-operative venture in the ministry of prayer by the
National Christian Education Council and the
Methodist Church Overseas Division

Published by:
National Christian Education Council
Robert Denholm House
Nutfield
Redhill RH1 4HW

British Library Cataloguing-in-Publication Data:
  Oceans of Prayer
  1. Christianity. Prayers
  I. Trenaman, David R.
  242'8

  ISBN 0-7197-0763-3

First published 1991
© 1991 National Christian Education Council

Typesetting by Avonset, Midsomer Norton, Bath
Printed in Great Britain by Staples Printers, Rochester

CONTENTS

PREFACE

On our front cover, canoes and other small craft are pulled up on a beach in Haiti. They have been used to bring food from the sea to nurture the local community. They symbolise the daily meeting of the people who sail them.

The prayers in this book are likewise a meeting place, but from a wider community: they arise out of the depths of a wide variety of experiences from many parts of the world. Their voices mingle in praise of our common Lord and in intercession for the world in which we all live.

Many were written for a particular occasion or publication, for instance the Prayer Manual/Handbook of the Methodist Church in Britain, or for orders of service focussing on the World Church. They were commissioned from Church leaders and lay people and some were written spontaneously in response to a particular situation. Yet their use goes beyond the particular denomination, place or time.

The symbol of the ocean is powerful. Oceans cover almost three-quarters of the earth's surface. They have no set boundaries. One ocean flows into another, constantly moving, cleansing and generating life. Water is a sign of birth, death and rebirth in baptism.

The ocean is not always calm and reminds us of those who risked their lives to carry the Gospel to other lands, some island to island, in small canoes like those on our cover. Communications are different now. Some of these prayers arrived by fax!

Working for a Mission agency, we are privileged to be at a centre of communication. Through reading and using these prayers, and knowing how they are valued by local churches already, we felt they could be used more widely. We are grateful to all those who have agreed that they should be included. Supplementary information and acknowledgements are on page 101.

Both of us have worked in Africa, one in Kenya, bounded by the Indian Ocean and the other in Nigeria by the Atlantic Ocean. We both have a sense of the vast expanses of water that link Christians in their local situation with one another across the world and of the God to whom all our prayers are offered.

Maureen Edwards and Jan S Pickard

Turning to God

INTRODUCTION

In the agony of the cross, Jesus prayed for the well-being of those who were responsible for his pain. In Christ, it is possible to turn to God in prayers of forgiveness, to work for reconciliation and peace. This has been revealed over and over again in the present conflict in Sri Lanka. Churches in Jaffna, Batticaloa and Colombo are full and overflowing. Even those on the fringes of the Church have turned to God, because, when all human resources fail, God is there. God alone gives sustenance and spiritual refreshment.

In 1983, the Methodist College compound was filled by about 500 men, women and children from all walks of life - they were Tamils, Christians and Hindus. They had come, driven by fear. Each one had a tale to tell. Their house was burned, their things looted; some had a loved one or more murdered. They all had the common experience of being threatened by Sinhala mobs. They were sad, afraid and uncertain about the future.

As the sun set and darkness crept in, some people naturally moved into the large Kollupitya Methodist Church in the centre of the compound. As singing was heard from the church, other Christians joined in worship, and then some Hindus came.

The Hindus at first were surprised to hear singing. What was there to sing about? There was killing, looting and burning all around, but no talk of revenge against the Sinhalese. The Rev Soma Perera, then President of the Methodist Church, spoke of forgiveness. He, a Sinhalese, asked forgiveness of Tamils for what had been done to them. He spoke of reconciliation and love.

Some Hindus found this difficult to understand. What makes a Christian turn to God in praise, thanksgiving and prayers for the forgiveness of those who caused such hurt? Instinctive turning to God for personal safety and protection, they could understand, for many could testify to God's saving power in the midst of calamity. But forgiveness? And joy in the midst of suffering and pain? Is this possible?

Love is not slurring over sin but actively seeking the good of the sinner. That is what the cross reveals. And this is the purpose of worship: in silence to become aware that God is love.

Rajah Jacob, Sri Lanka

PRESENCE

Come, Holy God,
Come, loving Source of our life,
Come, healing Light.

Come, healing Light,
Source of our life,
Come, healing Light.

India

Eternal God,
   you are the power that created the universe,
   the energy that fires everything,
   the strength that sustains our world.
Eternal Father,
   you are the love that encircles us,
   the grace that enables us,
   ' : truth that enlightens us.
Eiernal Saviour,
   you are the glory of the cross of Christ,
   the hope of the resurrection,
   the life of the Holy Spirit.
God of love, power and might.

Anne Knighton, United Kingdom

Great and merciful God
Your life is the source of the whole world's life;
Your mercy is our only hope;
Your eyes watch over all your creatures;
You know the secrets of our hearts.
By your life-giving Spirit, draw us into your presence,
That we may worship in the true life of your Spirit,
With lives moved by your love,
Through him who has led us to your heart of love,
Even Jesus Christ our Lord.

India

OCEANS OF PRAYER

Lord of all creation,
showing your glory in ever-changing matter,
who took flesh and blood
to body forth your presence,
may the very stones cry out your life and love.

Kenneth Street, United Kingdom

Lord, we are your people.
You have gathered us together
to share in your purpose
and advance your kingdom
of love, justice and peace.
In our worship and devotion
open our minds to know your will.

We come like people at the first Easter,
raised by Christ to be his presence in the world.
We come joyfully and gladly to offer praise and adoration
to the living God.
In the name of Jesus,
accept our praise.
We come to worship.
God is with us,
Christ our Saviour is raised from death to redeem us.
God's Holy Spirit is present to guide and encourage us.
In the name of Jesus,
accept our praise.

Kate Johnson, United Kingdom

Preparing ourselves for God's presence

We spend a few minutes allowing ourselves to relax
and become aware that God is present with us
and with all who have gathered.
We begin by being still.
We listen to the sounds around us, and acknowledge them.
We deepen our breathing.
We focus on God, quietly expressing our love.
We focus on those who have gathered with us,
praying for their renewal.
We focus on ourselves.

As we breathe out,
we imagine letting go of those thoughts,
wishes, words and actions which cut us off
from a full relationship with God.
As we breathe in,
we imagine letting in the gentle breeze of God's spirit
- all that is true and pure and lovely.
We breathe out.
We breathe in.
We are still.

Call to worship

You wait for us until we are open to you.
   We wait for your word to make us receptive.
Attune us to your voice, to your silence.
   Speak and bring your Son to us - Jesus, the word of your peace.

Australia

PRAISE AND THANKSGIVING

God of the galaxies
Yet accessible to every human heart;
Mind behind the universe
Yet one whom we can call our Father;
Infinite
Yet within our reach;
Awesome and majestic
Yet compassionate and tender;
Above and beyond us
Yet here beside us:
We praise your name
Through Jesus Christ our Lord.

John Platts, United Kingdom

OCEANS OF PRAYER

Praise be to you, O God, the origin of the universe,
by whose wisdom we are created and sustained.
Praise be to you, O God, the Father of our Lord Jesus Christ,
by whose love we are redeemed and forgiven.
Praise be to you, O God, the source of all holiness,
by whose spirit we are made whole and brought to perfection.
Praise be to you, O God, Father, Son and Holy Spirit,
for ever and ever.

Norman Wallwork, United Kingdom

We thank you, God!
We want to tell the world
what you have done:
your wonderful works.
We praise you, God!
We remember our beginnings
and celebrate belonging
together in your world.
We trust you, God!
You are still our help.
We go forward in faith
remembering all you have done.

Jan S Pickard

Jesus calls us, Jesus calls us today;
let us hear him, let us hear his true word;
let us thank him, for he gives us life.

Zambia

O God our Father, Creator of the universe,
whose majesty is unfathomed,
and whose greatness knows no bounds.
You are the Lord of glory,
whose love is unending and absolute
and whose grace is all-embracing.
You are the Supreme Matai* of all nations,
big and small,
of all peoples and all races.

Samoa

Family chief in Samoa

In a world in which there is so much hunger
we give thanks for food;
In a world in which there is so much loneliness
we give thanks for friends;
And in a world in which there is so much to do,
we ask for strength to spend ourselves in Christ's service.

United Kingdom

Living God, we give you thanks
for our fathers and mothers in the faith:
those who have revealed to us your grace in Christ
through their lives, preaching and in hymns.
Strengthen the fellowship of the Church,
and our sense of belonging to a worldwide family.

Gaspard Mensah, Togo

Laid up forever
   in the field of heaven
There glows the image
   of the Bethlehem stable,
Fled to the Star
   which led the Wise men there.
To Thee be glory
   carolling in anthem -
In thy great mystery
   all worship is de Babeled,
The tongues are mingled
   as they reach thine ear,
Sung in America
   or Mozambique or China.
And thou wilt answer
   on the wing of prayer -
So they be seen
   as singing just one carol
Whose notes are rays
   that centre on the Star.

A J Seymour, Guyana

OCEANS OF PRAYER

Jesus my Lord, you are depth,
Indeed my Lord you are depth:
Having no sin, yielding to no evil.
Your hands sweet and clean,
Yet you became the friend of sinners,
Your love freely shared among them.

Jesus my Lord, you are depth,
Indeed my Lord, you are depth:
For though you fed crowds upon crowds
Until they had had enough and to spare,
Yet you yourself suffered all the pangs of hunger
For forty days in the wilderness.

Jesus my Lord, you are depth,
Indeed my Lord, you are depth:
Loosing the chains of those who were bound
In body or in spirit,
Yet you yourself in chains went the dolorous way
From Gethsemane to Calvary.

Harcourt Whyte, Nigeria

Risen Lord, Saviour and Redeemer, we give thanks for your presence with us. For your unchanging love which reconciles and sets us free to worship,

   We praise and thank you, Lord.

For your faithful people of every age and culture who, through the power of your love, have proclaimed and shared the good news of the gospel,

   We praise and thank you, Lord.

For those who day by day build bridges in love, serve in humility and quietly share their faith without counting the cost,

   We praise and thank you, Lord.

Holy Spirit, guide, counsellor and friend, who leads us into all truth, for your love which recreates, renews and changes us to be more Christlike,

   We praise and thank you, Lord.

For ways in which your Spirit enlightens our ignorance, changes our ideas and thinking, and challenges us to seek new opportunities for mission and service,

   We praise and thank you, Lord.

Margaret Bethel, United Kingdom

Let us thank God that his Holy Spirit has been moving amongst us to open our hearts to him and to each other.
Amen

   Yes Lord, so says my heart.

Let us thank God that through misunderstanding and unfaithfulness he has brought us to this day of truth and joy.
Amen

   Yes Lord, so says my heart.

Forgive us, Father, that we have harboured suspicion and magnified hurts within your Church.
Amen

   Yes Lord, so says my heart.

Forgive us, Father, that we have been blinded by prejudice, careless in our conversation, quick to anger and slow to forgive.
Amen

   Yes Lord, so says my heart.

Forgive us, Father, as we do forgive all who have offended us.
Amen

   Yes Lord, so says my heart.

Christ Jesus came into the world to save sinners.
Hear then the word of grace:
'Your sins are forgiven'
Amen

   Yes Lord, so says my heart.

Praise be to you, O Lord, for you have filled our cup to overflowing.
Amen

   Yes Lord, so says my heart.

Praise be to you, O Lord, who in the power of your resurrection gives us confidence and hope for the future.
Amen

   Yes Lord, so says my heart.

Nigeria

Lord of all, Creator and Source of all life, you rule in strength and steadfast love over all the earth. Your glory shines through the lives and traditions of all people. Your love does not change:

The power and the glory are yours forever.

The destiny of every nation is in your hands: the achievements of great empires and their leaders come to an end, but you are worshipped in every age, by every generation, in every land. Your love does not change:

The power and the glory are yours forever.

In Christ's death and resurrection, you demonstrated the power of your kingdom to overcome evil. You move ahead of us, using forces and movements in the world, bringing reconciliation and healing. In you the powerless and weak find strength and courage. Your love does not change:

The power and the glory are yours forever.

We praise you for every sign of your power to save, the experience of 'the heart strangely warmed', for the change you have begun within us through your Spirit who leads us to repent and draws us closer together in the community of Christ's body. Your love does not change:

The power and the glory are yours forever.

Maureen Edwards

FOR OURSELVES

Our God and Father, we thank you that in Jesus Christ all may return to you and find their real identity. We thank you for the power of the Holy Spirit that brings us from ourselves to Christ. We rejoice in the privilege of belonging to the one Body of Christ and the fellowship of believers throughout the world.

Ghana

God, our Heavenly Father, we draw near to thee with thankful hearts because of all thy great love for us. We thank thee most of all for the gift of thy dear Son, in whom alone, we may be one. We are different from one another in race and language, in material things, in gifts, in opportunities, but each of us has a human heart, knowing joy and sorrow, pleasure and pain. We are one in our need of thy forgiveness, thy strength, thy love; make us one in our common response to thee, that bound by a common love and freed from selfish aims, we may work for the good of all and the advancement of thy Kingdom.

Queen Salote, Tonga

Lord God most high, we thank you for letting us hear your precious Gospel. We are happy to be called Christians, so make us all real ones. Cleanse our hearts and make them clear as crystals, so we may see you and the Holy Spirit may dwell in us.

Thailand

Lord Jesus Christ, the way, the truth and the life, we confess our slowness to love as you commanded. Forgive the poverty of our prayer life, our lack of diligence in studying your word, and our neglect of fellowship with our Christian brothers and sisters. Lord, forgive us. By the power of your love, change and renew us.

Margaret Bethel, United Kingdom

Lord, you give to us brother, sister, parent, child, friend, colleague, partner; you offer the possibility of rich, loving relationships. But we take one another for granted; we abuse and do not respect each other as we should. Father, forgive us,

and help us to be more aware of your way.

Lord, you offer us a new way of living, a supreme example to follow; but we are easily attracted by material things and lose sight of our goal. Father, forgive us,

and help us to be more aware of your way.

OCEANS OF PRAYER

Lord, you share with us all that you have. Yet we are reluctant to give you our 'all', because it is costly and painful. Your hands are open and ours are so often closed. Father, forgive us,

and help us to be more aware of your way.

Let us hear the words of assurance - our sins are forgiven.

Amen. Thanks be to God.

Rosemary Wass, United Kingdom

Living God, God of truth and grace, God of Cross and Resurrection;

We are blind to your presence in the world.
We have failed to live by your love;
we are weak and selfish and proud;
we need your Spirit within;
forgive us all our evil, in the name of Christ.

Our Saviour forgives all who see their great need;
all who turn to God, trusting God's grace as their aid;
God accepts you and frees you and calls you his friend;
believe, trust and live with Christ's peace to the end.

India

Today, good Lord, save me from being over anxious about the world's pains and tragedies, about the future of the Church, about the immediate challenges of life, about the ultimate future of all things and all lives. Teach me to trust in Christ, who carries the sins of the whole world, who is the Head of the Church, the Good Shepherd, the Resurrection and the Life, today and every day.

Richard G Jones, United Kingdom

For closed minds and prejudice, our unwillingness to change and failure to love,

Father forgive us.

For thinking we know best; for our unwillingness to listen and learn from people who come from other parts of the world,

Father forgive us.

For our neglect of you; for slackness in prayer; for not reading your word,

Father forgive us.

For our failure to witness for you, for trying to keep Jesus to ourselves and our friends in our local Church; for our lack of concern for the World Church,

Father forgive us.

Elsie Purbrick, United Kingdom

Father, you know what is in us. You come into the secret place, where we are alone in our minds, where no one else can come. You know our fears and anxieties, our feelings of guilt, inadequacy, despair. All this we bring to you.

Forgive and make us whole.

Father, we are relatively comfortable and perhaps because of this, we are often shy Christians, slow to witness, complacent about our spirituality, apathetic about working and giving for your Kingdom, altogether too easily satisfied. All this we bring to you.

Forgive and make us whole.

Rosemary Wakelin, United Kingdom

Lord, I am tired and afraid. Yet, Lord, I know my charge is simple: to love and serve you, to keep the faith, to spread your living kindness. Lord, give me the strength to continue in your service.

Sybil Phoenix, United Kingdom

OCEANS OF PRAYER

O my God save me;
in the midst of grave difficulties
which surround us
may I find my soul's peace;
I am seeking thy way.

Zaire

How can we believe in you, God, when we have to live in
uncertainty?
How can we trust you when we can see the smoke rising from
the volcano?
Women worry for the future of their children,
men anguish over the harvests which may not be.
Children cling to their parents for fear of the dark.
Where is your saving hand O God?
Where is your kindness and mercy?
When hardship and fear abound, you are there
in those who listen and take the strain.
Sharing and hospitality, self denial and benevolence
are the signs of your presence:

These will always be with us when you are with us,
these will always remain as long as your love remains.
Where are you, God, in the times of our troubles?
You are always with us in the good times and the bad.
You are always with us.

Janice Clark, United Kingdom

O Jesus,
Be the canoe that holds me up in the sea of life;
Be the rudder that keeps me on a straight course;
Be the outrigger that supports me in times of great temptation.
Let your Spirit be my sail that carries me through each day.
Keep my body strong, so I can paddle steadfastly on in the
voyage of life.

Melanesia

Lead us, Almighty God our Father,
from Death to Life,
from Falsehood to Truth.
Lead us, Lord and Saviour Jesus Christ,
from Despair to Hope,
from Fear to Trust.
Lead us, Divine Holy Spirit,
from Hatred to Love,
from War to Peace.
Let your Peace fill our Hearts, our Homes,
our Community, our Country,
our World, our whole Universe.
For the sake of the one who made peace
by the blood of his Cross, Jesus Christ our Lord.

Ivan McElhinney, Ireland

'I have written your name on the palms of my hands' *(Isaiah 49.16)*
Lord, we know our own names:
labelled, passported, well documented:
we know who we are and where we are going.
But we are still anxious, restless,
constantly checking our labels:
do we know who we are
and where we are going?
You do not label us, but call us by name,
love us, and hold our lives in your hand:
help us to know we are loved
and to trust in you as we go.

Jan S Pickard

O God,
make me a human who is
strong-minded
imaginative
level-headed
sympathetic
a human who knows his/her mind
and is not afraid to speak it.

Henry Victor, Sri Lanka

OCEANS OF PRAYER

God of change and constant love, we thank you that you lead
us in new and unexpected ways, with a strong arm and a
guiding hand.
Give your people unity in diversity, and courage to change.

Wycherley Gumbs, Caribbean

O God, who art the unsearchable abyss of peace,
   the ineffable sea of love, the fountain of blessings
   and the bestower of affection,
   who sendest peace to those that receive it;
Open to us this day the sea of thy love
   and water us with plenteous streams
   from the riches of thy grace
   and from the most sweet springs of thy kindness.
Make us children of quietness and heirs of peace,
   enkindle in us the fire of thy love;
   sow in us thy fear;
   strengthen our weakness by thy power;
   bind us closely to thee and to each other
   in our firm and indissoluble bond of unity.

Syria

Give us, Lord, that holy fire
to renew us day by day;
may we have that warmth in us
to proclaim your love and power.

Gershon Anderson, Sierra Leone

Let my heart always think of him.
Let my head always bow down to him.
Let my lips always sing his praise.
Let my hands always worship him.
Let my body always serve him with love.
O Lord of grace, immense like a mountain peak,
   full of goodness!
Do thou forgive my sins!
When my spirit leaves my body,
let me behold thy Divine face,
   radiant like the lotus,
even on the cross on which thine enemies nailed thee,
and let my heart rejoice in thy sacred name.
Grant thou this boon to me O Lord!

Krishna Pillai, India

O Almighty God, I humbly ask thee to make me like a tree planted by the waterside, that I may bring forth fruits of good living in due season. Forgive my past offences, sanctify me now, and direct all that I should be in the future, for Christ's sake.

Nigeria

For all the blessings and needs we have named and the many more unnamed but known to you, God we thank you and pray that you hear us when we call on you.
O God, we pray you, fill your servants with your Holy Spirit, that the works we undertake may be redemptive, our words prophetic and our worship meaningful. Inspire us with your love, challenge us with your truth and empower us with your strength.

Mercy A Oduyoye, WCC

Dear God,
I offer myself to you:
my mind - to think for you;
my eyes - to see the needs of others;
my ears - to hear the world's cries;
my voice - to speak for you;
my hands - to work for your Kingdom;
my feet - to walk in your path;
my life - to be used in your service;
my heart - to love you above all.
May the joy of the Lord be my strength.

United Kingdom

BEYOND OURSELVES

God, our Father, Creator of the world and King of the universe, we give you thanks for our very life and the living that our world makes possible. We crave your pardon for our misdeeds. We plead for mercy and forgiveness. We need to know you more, to love and serve you better and love our neighbours as ourselves. Give grace we beseech you to our leaders in the Church and the State. Grant them wisdom and a deeper insight of your love. May they look to you for guidance. Bless our country and people; be unto us a tower of strength. May your will be done in our hearts and minds and hands.

Gershon Anderson, Sierra Leone

Lord, give strength to those who seek to serve you
and your Kingdom on earth;
give grace to those who would show the needy
your saving power in the land;
give love to those who would share
the glory of the suffering servant Jesus Christ
in peoples' lives.
For yours is the Kingdom and the power and the glory.

Jimmy Palos, Southern Africa

MEDITATIONS

Two streams met
and looked ahead at a vast desert.
The trees were dry and withered:
nothing grew; the mouths of the cattle were chapped:
everything was dry, awful.
The first said to the second, 'What are you going to do?'
The second stream travelled to the desert.
The desert said, 'I am going to swallow you.
There will be no change,
for I am glad when everything is dry, withered and dead.'
The second stream flowed on.
The desert opened its mouth
swallowed the stream
and remained a desert.

The first stream shook its head,
turned right round,
passed boulders,
went on up, up,
reached the infinite lake
which looked at the stream and said,
'I have long looked for a channel.'
The stream said,
'Pour through me.'

The lake poured through the stream.
The desert said, 'I will drink you up.'
The little stream flowed on and on
and swallowed up the desert.
And all the barren land
blossomed like a rose.

Ephraim Alphonse, Panama

Great reconciler of the divided,
Great leader leading us, great blanket around us:
Your hands are wounded, your feet are bruised.
Your blood pours forth - and why?
Your blood was shed for us.

Ntsikana, Southern Africa

If you mean to pray,
   don't make a display,
   adopting a pose
   in a public way,
   if you mean to pray.

Your father knows
   how everything goes -
   whatever you need,
   your joys and woes
   your father knows.

It must succeed,
   whenever you plead,
   and seek his will
   in word and deed,
   it must succeed.

Be calm and still
   before him, till
   you know his way.
   In good or ill,
   be calm and still.

It's time to pray,
   tonight, today,
   and every hour
   of every day:
   it's time to pray.

He has the power
   that can devour
   the raging wrong.
   Our truth and tower,
   he has the power.

Hugh Thomas, United Kingdom

OCEANS OF PRAYER

We must be a praying people.
We must beat against the doors of heaven,
   but even more we must make our hearts
   the meeting place
   between our sinful weakness
   and the resources of God.

Peter Storey, Southern Africa

It was raining outside.
I was alone in a foreign city.
Beside the hotel window I stood
and reflected on my country.
What is the destiny of my people?

   The people of Korea:
   in each of them I see
   the mysterious presence of our Lord.
   Through the wet glass of the window
   his face is seen dimly.

He is being crucified.
There are spots of blood
and his body is bruised.
And even in his suffering he
is the glory of the risen Lord.

Scattered small flowers
   surround him with graceful dew.

Hong Chong Myung, Korea

Wilderness
Place of withdrawal
Spirit
God within
Willing extraction
from the world
pressing
round the rim
of isolation
giving meaning
asking questions
demanding answers.

28

Place of stripping
Spirit
God within
Sand-lashing wind
stinging face
and heart
whipping
round the dunes
of desolation
baring self-deceit
cleansing vision
scouring pride.

Place of exposure
Spirit
God within
Scattering security
in emptiness
removing
signposts to certainty
feeling bare
standing alone
setting free.

Place of glory
Spirit
God within
sun-blazing light
illuminating
depths of darkness
surprising
the landscape of living
with rainbows
stimulating hope
showing direction
strengthening resolve.

Betty Hares, United Kingdom

OCEANS OF PRAYER

Lord, I want to grow.
Not in my body, since I know you said
no worrying or working could do that.

No, Lord, I want to grow
spiritually.
I want to pray much better,
to read the Bible more,
with deeper insights, and to share
the things I find with others
not as blessed as me;
to know how to speak
more fluently of you,
and, too, to preach in golden words
that will compel belief.
And all this, naturally,
to your great glory . . .

Lord, I want me to grow.
You brought me here
to meet with people from across the world.
You taught me that first day
a stranger can be homesick -
want to talk of family and child.
You showed me that a different skin from mine
hides humour, shyness, love,
and these reach out to find the same in me.
And that far-off disaster on the news
matters to one with whom
I washed up yesterday.
You show me here
longings for freedom and the exile's pain.
You make me share the stranger's puzzlement,
frustration, joy . . .

You want me, Lord, to grow
in love, only in mankind.
You teach that truth
is not confined to those
who think and look and talk like me.

You want in me no tough, ascetic Antony,
nor Chrysostom, the gold-tongued preacher;
no Luther, Wesley, changing history's course,
but Christ,
your love made flesh
to be made flesh in me.

You want me, Lord, to grow
only in love.

Peter Russell, United Kingdom

Sharing in Suffering and Struggle

INTRODUCTION

Our Lord Jesus Christ spent all night on bended knee in the Garden of Gethsemane, the arena of his suffering and struggle, to make one request of his Father, 'May your will be done'.

To pray like Jesus is to die to self and become truly alive to his teachings in the Gospel. It is to pray with power and conviction. It is to pray earnestly and effectively. It is to pray without ceasing *(1 Thessalonians 5.17)*.

Our participation in suffering and struggle demands that we must never cease to pray, so as to overcome every kind of obstacle and discouragement. It demands our time, our concentration and our persistence to persevere.

Our participation in suffering and struggle is a call to self-sacrifice, a price which must be daily paid. We cannot evade the cross. Scars are the authentic marks of committed and faithful discipleship, the signs of Jesus' own suffering and struggle.

Our participation in suffering and struggle is a challenge to 'rise' with Jesus, overcoming mountains of rejection, mountains of pain, mountains of sorrow, mountains of resentment, mountains of misunderstandings, mountains of misrepresentations, mountains of problems, mountains of oppression, mountains of difficulties, mountains of setbacks, mountains of anxieties. This is the victory - the sign of Jesus' resurrection over the forces of evil and death.

Pray to move mountains, inspired by God in and through the power of the Holy Spirit.

Pray to move mountains, inspired by faith that the unknown may be known and the unexperienced experienced. Many were they who by faith conquered kingdoms, performed acts of righteousness, obtained promises, shut the mouths of lions, quenched the power of fire, escaped the edge of the sword, and from weakness were made strong *(Hebrews 11)*.

Yes, in suffering and struggle, we 'have this treasure in earthen vessels, that the surprising greatness of the power may be of God and not from ourselves;
we are afflicted in every way, but not crushed;
perplexed, but not despairing;
persecuted, but not forsaken;
struck down, but not destroyed;
always carrying about in the body the dying of Jesus, that the life of Jesus may also be manifested in our body'.

(2 Corinthians 4.7-9)

Lesley G Anderson, Panama

PRESENCE

We talk of 'living in Christ with people' - what people?
We have torn ourselves apart from the rest of our body.
Lest you turn aside from us,
we reach out our hands to grasp our severed limbs,
we reach out to the unloved, the unwashed, the ulcerated.
We reach out to those imprisoned: imprisoned behind bars,
imprisoned behind masks, imprisoned in endless labour.
We reach out to those who sell their bodies for money;
or sell their children for money;
or sell their country for money.
With reluctance we reach out to those who crucify us,
the powerful, the oppressors, the rich.
Come, bone of our bones, flesh of our flesh,
join with us, make us whole again!
Spirit of the living God, come,
put breath in us and bring us to life,
cleanse us, renew us, empower us.
In the name of Christ, in whom alone we are complete.

Asia

You are the God of the poor, the human and simple God, the
God who sweats in the street, the God with a weather-beaten
face. That's why I talk to you in the way that my people talk,
because you are the labourer God, the worker Christ.

Nicaragua

Oh Lord, we present our prayers before you as a fragrant
offering,
we join our hearts in prayer and praise,
we pray that we may experience your peace in our hearts;
we pray for peace throughout the world;
we pray for the deeds of love of your holy Church;
and for all the people gathered together
as your Church throughout the world.

Yukio Yokoyama, Japan

Somewhere in this
hopeless whirlpool of life -
a hand extends to help.

Woon Lai Eng, Singapore

PRAISE AND THANKSGIVING

Jesus answered, 'Go and tell John what you hear and see: the blind recover their sight, the lame walk, the lepers are made clean, the deaf hear, the dead are raised to life, the poor are hearing the good news. . .'

In India, women chosen from the village walk many miles to receive training in basic health-care and transform the lives of their fellow villagers. For each sign of the coming of God's kingdom:

Let us rejoice and be glad.

The great scourge of smallpox has been eliminated from this planet. For each sign of the coming of God's kingdom:

Let us rejoice and be glad.

The use of a simple and effective treatment for dehydration is spreading world-wide. For each sign of the coming of God's kingdom:

Let us rejoice and be glad.

Christa Hook, United Kingdom

Our loving Father, and Father of ALL
We thank you for having brought us together
in this land to learn to love you
and one another.

We thank you for our Church with
its diverse membership.
We know, Gracious Father, that we have
not always been obedient to you.

Give us courage, we pray, to stand up
for your truth.
Make us apostles of your love, justice,
hope, reconciliation and peace.

We ask all these in his name,
the Prince of Peace,
our Lord and Master, Jesus Christ.

Stanley Mogoba, Southern Africa

FOR OURSELVES

O God, who has given us the grace to carry the sword of your Kingdom of peace, who has made us messengers of peace in a world of strife, and messengers of strife in a world of false peace: make strong our hand, make clear our voice, give us humility with firmness and insight with passion, that we may fight not to conquer, but to redeem.

Tonga

Rescue us, O Lord.
We are sinking in deep marsh,
We have no place to stand any more.
We find ourselves in deep water,
the waves devour us.
We have cried till we are exhausted,
our throats are gaping wounds.
Our eyes are inflamed,
because we have looked for help for so long . . .

The insults hurled against us
are hurled against you also,
because you created everyone
in your own image . . .

Praise the Lord, you who are suffering,
for he will give back what belongs to you,
to your children and to your children's children.

Centlivres Karuaera, Namibia

Lord, like Peter we want to follow you,
but are afraid of the cost.
How much time do you want? How much caring?
How much thinking and wrestling with our conscience?
How many of our possessions are required in your service?
Where is your peace to be found?

Peace grows through closeness to God
in our response to his will for us in living and loving.
In many situations it means costly giving
that is alight with
his peace and joy.

Stella Jefferies, United Kingdom

OCEANS OF PRAYER

Prayer with Christians in the Middle East

'The wounds of the suffering are our wounds'
We pray for the places
so often in the news
that we may not become numbed
to the hurt of their people,
baffled by the complexity
of their problems,
and forget that Christ
is not the name of a faction
but suffers with all humanity.

Jan S Pickard

We confess the times we have denied the power of your love,
and sought our own power through manipulation and
domination.
Forgive us

and fill us with your love.

We confess the times we have not witnessed for your love and
truth,
but followed blindly the powerful of the world,
though they have led us into ways of injustice, fear and conflict.
Forgive us

and fill us with your love.

We confess the times we have despised the weak and
powerless:
times we have exploited, or just ignored them.
Forgive us

and fill us with your love.

(Silent prayer)

Dear Lord, enable us
to know your forgiveness,
understand your grace,
and be filled with your love and power.

Anne Knighton, United Kingdom

SHARING IN SUFFERING AND STRUGGLE

Father God, I thank you for this new day.
Forgive me for all the pain
I caused you and others yesterday.
Through what was done to me by my friends and neighbours,
the hurt just would not go away.
I pray you Father, change me and enable me to forgive.
Take away the pain and put a loving spirit in me.
Father, I trust you through the victory
and the power of the cross,
its length, its breadth, its height, its depth.
As you gave yourself to gain my soul,
change me into a forgiving person
and set me free to love all my neighbours and friends.
Widen my vision, not just to stay on the mountain top,
but, Jesus, as you took your disciples down to ground level
to see other visions,
help me to face the issues before me.
Strengthen me in power and give me your inward peace,
for I am yours, O Father.
I know that you can make me whole again,
through your love for me.

Sybil Phoenix, United Kingdom

Show forth your power, O Lord of the nations,
and do a new thing among your people
and establish justice, peace and true community.

Our hearts are heavy, our wounds are deep;
do not wait, O Lord, but bring your healing
before we can no longer forgive;
before, consumed with hatred,
we lose the ability to love.
When death had done its worst,
you brought your Son to new life.
You revealed the power of your love
and your victory over evil.
Break our bonds and set us all free
that we may know that you are the Lord.

Southern Africa

OCEANS OF PRAYER

My body is paralysed.
By God's strength someday I will be free.
When that day comes I will be filled with joy.
   This I know.
I haven't walked from the day I was born,
On the warm backs of my parents and brothers and sisters
I can go anywhere.
   This I know.
I am unable to speak.
I cannot speak gossip
Or speak harsh words.
   This I know.
In the midst of sorrow and pain
There is joy and happiness.
In the midst of this, I am alive.
   This I know.

Kumi Hayashi, Japan

God, who has given us grace
to be instruments of love in its work
of healing and judgement,
who has commissioned us to proclaim forgiveness
and condemnation,
deliverance to the captive and captivity to the proud:
give us the patience of those who understand,
and the impatience of those who love;
that the might of your gentleness may work through us,
and the mercy of your wrath may speak through us.

Tonga

Our Father, we ask your guidance and wisdom in learning to
discern your will. Help us not to lose hope when overwhelmed
by the enormity of poverty, hunger and oppression among our
people. And give us the courage to work towards your justice
wherever we live, so that your kingdom on earth may become
a reality.

Lesley Anderson, Panama

SHARING IN SUFFERING AND STRUGGLE

O God
Our suffering sigh in heaven is heard
and faith in you will ease all pain.
We shall not give up!

O Christ Jesus,
We know that you are alive in all of us.
You strengthen us by your own journey to Calvary.
We shall not give up!

O Holy Spirit,
You give us hope and courage.
We shall not give up!
We shall continue to live in hope.
Help us in our struggles for daily bread;
Help us in our struggles for justice and peace.

Gershon Anderson, Sierra Leone

BEYOND OURSELVES

O God, bless those who are burdened with cares.
May they find new life, rest and refreshment in you.
O God, however hard their circumstances,
help them to discern the truth
and see that their lives can be changed
through the love of Christ our Lord . . .
O God, when depression takes hold,
encourage them with your inner truths,
so that they can know the fullness of life.
O God, in the struggle of life
may they know that you are their very present help in trouble.
Lord Jesus, you spoke to the world
through your own suffering and triumph;
speak to us now through the sufferings, triumphs and hopes
of our sisters and brothers.

Joyce Hastings, United Kingdom

OCEANS OF PRAYER

Father God, we are aware that while our life may be comfortable or protected, many of your family have no homes, no jobs and not enough food. Show us how to share all that we enjoy through the channels open to us in the life and work of your Church.

Father God, we are blessed with real fellowship. The Church is a worshipping community and in it we are free to express our devotion. Yet in many areas of the world, to worship openly brings persecution and harassment. Strengthen through your Holy Spirit those who dare to witness in face of hostility and misunderstanding.

Father God, we live in families and communities that provide care and support in joy and sorrow. We think of families that live with tension, political unrest or in fear of neighbours.

We pray that through your Church, the Body of Christ, your love may be shown in justice and peace. Help us to be faithful witnesses.

Stella Jefferies, United Kingdom

God of our daily lives
we pray for the people of the cities of this world
working and without work;
homeless and well housed;
fulfilled or frustrated;
confused and cluttered with material goods,
or scraping a living from others' leavings;
angrily scrawling on walls,
or reading the writing on the wall;
lonely or living in community;
finding their own space
and respecting the space of others.
We pray for our sisters and brothers,
mourning and celebrating -
may we share their suffering and hope.

Jan S Pickard

Jehovah! Great I AM, who was and is and is to be,
hear in love the cry of your people for life.
Your people need bread -
but grant that amid hard realities and hunger
we may understand that we do not live by bread alone.
Give to our leaders true wisdom;
save us all from economic, moral and social decay.
May your Church, with the gift of the Spirit,
rightly discern the things that make for peace,
for survival, and more -
for life in all its fullness:
and may we be bold to speak your word.

Franklin Roberts, Caribbean

Let us pray for the world-wide church:
For all who seek to bring health and healing to the sick in our
hospitals and in hospitals everywhere; for all who serve our
community as doctors, health visitors and district nurses; for all
involved in community-health projects in every part of the
world,

Lord, hear our prayer.

For all who work amongst the poor in every society, with the
homeless and refugees, the unemployed and migrants seeking
employment; for all who serve the handicapped, the distressed
and those isolated by their society,

Lord, hear our prayer.

For all who work to improve farming methods and crops, to
increase irrigation and prevent soil erosion; for all who enable,
through the development of industry, the growth of skills and
opportunities for self-reliance,

Lord, hear our prayer.

Elizabeth Bellamy, United Kingdom

OCEANS OF PRAYER

We pray for those who are suffering this day from hunger, poor housing, unemployment, loneliness and despair as a result of neglect and injustice; may their spirits not be broken by their bodies' pain; may the ministry amongst the people in pain be one of hope and peace; may they discover new skills and direction in their daily lives.

Jesus Christ, friend of the poor and lonely, we give you thanks for the opportunity to share the lives of people who are neglected by society, whose lives are burdened by circumstances beyond their control. We pray that our ministry may bring comfort and hope to these people in need as we seek your Kingdom of peace on earth.

Jimmy Palos, Southern Africa

God of power and of the poor
we rejoice at the growing role of women in society; we confess that they are still oppressed, that with children they are still hardest hit by poverty.
We rejoice that in some communities human dignity is affirmed; but we confess that in many places people are persecuted in their search for basic rights; food, shelter, employment.
We rejoice that the Churches are speaking out together against apartheid; but we confess the role of our leaders in supporting oppressive governments.
We rejoice in the generous response of people of all faiths to the African crisis; we are concerned that many people, throughout the world, are still hungry.

United States of America

Prayer with Asia

The city is new and strange to many people:
it beckons and promises.
There are lights at night
and shops and excitement.
Full of hope, men and women
bring their children from the village,
the paddy field, the dawn forest:
and they find concrete and asphalt,

low paid work on the assembly line
and a home in tenement or shanty town.
It is hard to keep human dignity
in urban society
where the skill and wisdom of the village
have no place.
Lord, may the strangers in the city
know you are by their side.

Jan S Pickard

God, our guide,
we live in hope for the future:
we are determined to go on,
to venture
with the help of our partners,
making great efforts,
so that 'those who were no people'
may truly become your people.
Difficult days lie ahead,
but we believe that in the end,
with your help,
we shall overcome.

Alain Rocourt, Haiti

Your reign is Life
Your reign is Truth
Your reign is Justice
Your reign is Peace
Your reign is Grace
Your reign is Love

Come to us our Lord and King.

He will free the poor who beseech,
The innocent who has no protection,
He will have mercy upon the humble and poor,
And he will save their lives from violence
Because his blood is precious to their eyes.

OCEANS OF PRAYER

Let the mountains bring peace
Let the hills bring justice
Let him be a blessing to his people
Let the nations proclaim his name
Let him defend the humble of the people
and defeat the exploiter.

Let your justice run over the earth
Let your Kingdom come, O Lord
Let the poor see the light of total liberation.
The yoke of oppression will be broken
and the hungry will be filled with bread.

Latin America

O Lord God of history, give us wisdom and power to build a
new society,
a society where justice and peace shall reign,
where violence and torture are unknown,
where there are no detainees and no suffering.
We pray for democratic systems of government
under which human rights are respected
and all can live safely in their own homes;
under which workers will be treated with respect
and paid a fair wage.
We are nations divided by politics
- we pray anxiously for unity;
free us from external pressures
- we pray for true independence in the world.
Hear our prayers, O Lord, and be our source of hope,
in the name of Jesus.

Korea

We pray for the victims of war and for those who profit by war
- the nations who produce and sell ever more sophisticated
weapons; we pray for those who use them to fight and kill.
Forgive them for their trade in human blood. Show them a
better way of living, make them and us more sensitive to each
other, more aware of your image in each human being.

We put our trust in you. We need your tree of life to heal our
suffering, to feed every nation with your fruits of justice, love
and peace. May your kingdom come in our lives.

Mozambique

We remember all who are held hostage
by armed men
or by history;
by politics based on a balance of terror,
by their own fears and prejudices.
We remember families who are separated
and people who are exiled
from the land of their birth
by frontiers, by barbed wire,
by divisions in the minds of men and women.
We remember places long held as holy
by people of different faiths
which have become territory
to be fought over, their names
meaning suffering - modern Golgothas.
We pray for redemption -
for prisoners, for victims of injustice,
for our common humanity.

Jan S Pickard

Loving God, we pray for all whose life is a daily routine of pain and suffering: for those who suffer illness at home or in hospital; for those who cannot enjoy life because they are poor, hungry or homeless. Prosper the work of all who are involved in the ministry of healing and make their zeal a challenge to others. Lord in your mercy,

Hear our prayer.

Loving God, we pray for all who are surrounded by hatred and anger; for those whose family life is threatened by breakdown; for these living in areas of the world where racial, tribal and national differences cause tension and stress. Break down, O Lord, the walls which separate your people. May peace and justice prevail. Lord in your mercy,

Hear our prayer.

George and Elaine Mulrain, Caribbean

Lord, the storm is done.
We could not keep it from coming;
we could not drive it away.
It came as a thief in the night.
Some were sleeping, Lord;
Heal them.
Raise them from the dead.
Some were at work.
Take away their fright.
Give them courage to pick up broken pieces.
The people are close to one another.
Foes are now friends.
Men have been tender.
Women have been brave.
Children have kept their faith.
Youth have matured in the storm.
It is a new people, Lord,
and they are calling on your name.
Hear us as we huddle together, Christ.
Be in our midst
as storms come and leave us.
Tell the wild winds to be still, Christ.
Tell them to be still.

Herbert Brokering, Caribbean.

MEDITATIONS

The Child in the Temple

Don't talk to us
of reconciliation
'. . . the Government's the enemy'
'. . . the terrorists can only terrorise'
We cannot accept half measures.
Don't look at us in surprise.

The child saw the reasons
for the political ideals . . .
He understood the urge to
purge the vice of terrorism . . .
And so he asked the question,
'Who will put love first?'

46

The answers came,
'I love my country'
'I love my neighbour'
'We are not guilty
of lack of love.'

'Who loves the children then -
both today's and tomorrow's?
Who creates community
rather than struggling in a fearful situation?'

'I want a peaceful land'
'I'm seeking peace and pursuing it'
'But you must hold it in your
hand, this peace, as you would
hold the hand of a child.
The body is the temple.
Touch each other's children,
then answer of your love.'

The temple courts were silent
- the crowd began to melt away.
Each harboured love in tension-clenched fists
and all the while the open palm
of love remained unshared.
The child's eyes misted over -
the parents had lost the child.

Stewart Morris, Ireland

Jesus you were executed on a cross.
You had no army, no resources,
no connections with the elite.

My heart is trembling.
Couldn't you have declared yourself
ruler of the earth?
Why didn't you establish the Kingdom?

Why these millions of bitter sighs?
Why these tears of angers, and broken hopes?
Why that naked despair in the eyes
of the little boy - my boy -
as he tried to escape the machine guns?

OCEANS OF PRAYER

It is as if you were not risen,
as if the promise were not ours,
as if we had to be afraid,
as if your power were not present
in our weakness.

And yet, are we not sharing in your Cross?
Are we not with you in your rejection?
And are we not beginning to live in
God's acceptance?
And can we not express your love
through our pain?

Southern Africa

Pieta

Your work accomplished,
now I know the sharpness of the sword
that pierces my heart through.
Again I hold you in my arms,
caress and kiss
that dearest form
which carried all my love.
But as I watched you grow
I knew
the life in you I nurtured
had a purpose I found hard to bear -
for you were mine and yet not mine,
for, though you loved me
as my dearest son,
I knew your being drew
its inner life
from the mysterious One
you called your Father;
and as you taught and healed
and blessed,
his love in you
embraced all humankind.

I touch your wounded feet
which walked the way
that led you to the cross.

SHARING IN SUFFERING AND STRUGGLE

I kiss your silent lips
which spoke the truth
the powerful still reject.

I feel the stillness
of your lifeless heart and know
the light of life itself has died.

The piercing grief
and weight of total loss
are now commensurate
with the joy I knew
in this my dearest love.

Now others wrap you round
and lay you
in your waiting tomb -

And waiting
night and day
and night
until I feel the stirring
in that earthy womb,
and pain and grief
and loss and death,
which laboured in you
for your victory
give birth
to Life and Truth,
your living Way,
and break out in the glory
of your Easter Day.

Rosemary Wakelin, United Kingdom

Lord, from our imperfect understanding of their suffering, we dare to stand with our brothers and sisters and pray with them.

We pray with children who, still and quiet from hunger, neither laughing nor crying, neither running nor resting, know little of life but hunger and waiting.

We pray with young women, bearing and nurturing the next generation. We pray for strength throughout pregnancy, safety in childbirth and joy in being the channel of life and love for each precious new being.

OCEANS OF PRAYER

We pray with men who, once strong and now weakened by chronic ill-health, struggle to go on working in mines, factories and on the land, made ill by the very conditions which they dare not leave.

(Silence)

Lord, in whose incarnation we see your deep involvement in all the complexities and greyness of living, we stand in shame with those who, by thoughtlessness or greed, have caused the ill-health or distress of others.

We pray with trained healers, who, for money or status, connive to retain the mystique of their profession, so that ordinary people never learn their skills.

We pray for farmers who grow destructive cash crops instead of the food people need; that your good earth may support life and not destroy it.

We pray with those involved in large firms selling useless or harmful medicines, which further impoverish those already poor.

We, who often benefit from the low wages paid to others, pray for justice in international trade.

(Silence)

Lord, we are glad to be associated with those who work in your healing mission. We pray with them.

We pray with all loving parents and sisters and brothers who cherish and heal in their own families.

We pray with those who, loving the lovely and the unlovely among those they know well, bring knowledge and wholeness to their own community.

We pray with the many agencies, Christian and secular, who work with individuals bringing healing; with communities encouraging self-reliance and co-operation; with governments planning health programmes, and interpreting the real needs of the silent poor.

(Silence)

Christa Hook, United Kingdom

In an African village,
a child of five
comes quietly to the door.
Her baby brother died yesterday.
As we enter,
the house is not silent
but full of people:
friends,
relatives,
neighbours have come in
to care for the bereaved family,
to be with them,
cook for them . . .
to listen, over and over again
to their grief . . .
to talk with them,
sing, pray and be silent . . .

They stay for days,
giving their time,
to bring comfort.
'Happy are those who mourn . . .'

Maureen Edwards

If I had not suffered
I would not have known the love of God.

If many people had not suffered
God's love would not have passed on.

If Jesus had not suffered
God's love would not have been made visible.

Mizuno Genzo, Japan

The Earth is
The Lord's

INTRODUCTION

Every human being has arrived in a mysterious manner into our planet earth. We do not remember where we have come from but, as in the parable of the mustard seed *(Mark 4.30-32)*, we arrive: miraculous, humble, weak, little babies. In many cultures of Africa, a baby's arrival is welcomed with gladness. It is seen as a blessing, a continuation, a hope of someone to carry the work of 'looking after'. Each one of us then, in such language, is a blessing, a sign of the continuation of creation, begun 'in the beginning . . . when the world was without form'. *(Genesis 1.1-2)*

In our time of prayer, we come face to face with the beautiful handiwork of God and are humbled by its welcoming nature to us. Our needs are met here, from the combination of gasses we breathe to food and shelter. Time for prayer is a time of truth, when we remove the 'blinders' of busy lives that lead us into the illusion that all is familiar and we are owners of the earth.

The Lord, whose history stretches from before our beginning and past our end, created the earth. He is the rightful owner. The mystery is that he, whose nature it is to be gracious, has invited us to participate in his world allowing us to call it home. And because we are not visitors, we have been allowed to 'move furniture', planting, pulling down, building up.

God has trusted us with his precious creation, and we have proved to be untrustworthy. Our arrogance, abuse and violation of the resources has made the earth a hostile place for other people as well as other life-forms.

Jesus enters our lives with a call to repent *(Mark 1.15)*: to turn from lifestyles which encourage the illusion of human owner-ship. It is our home only because God has been gracious to us. We, in turn, pray to be gracious to God in caring for the earth our home so that every human baby will always be celebrated as a blessing to the rest of creation.

R. Grace Imathiu, Kenya

PRESENCE

To the Holy Spirit

In the beginning
you gave life and movement,
colour and harmony
to the universe.
Everything moves by your power
and is one through you.
But most of all you move
in the minds and spirits
of men and women.
You give vision and insight,
speaking spirit to spirit.
You stir the sleeping conscience,
rouse the dormant mind,
to seek justice,
express beauty,
declare truth.
Most of all you come
in the power of Jesus,
bringing
love and joy and peace,
patience, kindness, goodness,
faithfulness, gentleness, self-control.
So move us now
in mind and conscience;
stir and quicken us
with beauty and truth;
and give us all your harvest,
now and always.

Hugh Thomas, United Kingdom

Prayer to the Great Spirit

Great Spirit, whose voice I hear in the winds
And whose breath gives life to all the world,
hear me!
I come before you, one of your many children.
I am small and weak,
I need your strength and wisdom.
Let me walk in beauty,

make my eyes ever behold the red and purple sunset.
Make my hands respect things
you have made.
Make my ears sharp to hear your voice -
Make me wise so that I may learn the things
you have taught my people.
Let me learn the lesson hidden in every leaf and rock -
I seek strength not to be greater than my brother or sister,
but to fight my greatest enemy - myself.
Make me ever ready to come to you
with clean hands and straight eyes
So that when life fades with the fading sunset
My spirit may come to you without shame.

Chi-meegwetch, Canada

May your Holy Spirit brood upon the islands of the world, and
bring peace, joy and justice.

Rajah Jacob. Sri Lanka

PRAISE AND THANKSGIVING

Who can forthtell the glory of your face?
The wonder of creation comes from you:
the majesty and awesome grandeur
of earth and sky.
Oh that my tongue could tell
the paradise of praise.

You are worthy of all honour, gracious God.
My eyes can see your greatness writ on high:
the stars, the sun and moon.
Words defy me as I try
to speak what my heart says.

If all the tongues of the earth should praise you,
joining as one in adoration,
then should we hear
the music of angels
and truly feel the power of your ways!

Jean Owen, United Kingdom

Gracious God, we give thanks for all you have given.
For the universe:
let our wonder grow.
For this world:
teach us better stewardship of earth and sea and sky.
For people everywhere:
let us see your image in every human face,
discern your hand in every human culture,
hear your voice in the silence
as well as the talk of neighbours.
For our Saviour, Christ, is at work in his world.

Australia

'. . . to hear thy loving kindness in the morning . . .'

Thank God for life, for living
Thank God for love, for giving
Thank God for death:
an ending a beginning.

Thank God for lips, for speaking
Thank God for hearts, for seeking
Thank God for weakness
a stumbling an upsurging.

Thank God for eyes for seeing
Thank God for soul, for being
Thank God for absence:
a longing an unfolding.

Thank God for life, for loving
Thank God for death, for longing
Thank him with singing.

Mary E Morgan, Caribbean

God, our Father and our Mother, creator and sustainer of the
universe, we thank you for the wondrous ways in which you
have revealed your love to us through the teachings of the sages
of India, wise men of the East; through the enlightened words
of the Buddha and the disciplined words of the Prophet
Mohammed, and through the light of the Gospel of Jesus
Christ. We pray that you will pour your love into our hearts that
with open minds we may accept all peoples of the world as
brothers and sisters, and serve them in true humility, so that all
humankind may find the joy of true freedom in you.

Rajah Jacob, Sri Lanka

Creator God, we thank you for the beauties of nature, for shape and colour; for times and seasons; for our dependence upon the earth and our responsibility as its stewards; for our care of animals and plants and for all signs of new life at this time of year. Creator of the Universe,

We thank you.

Creator God, we thank you for giving birth to the human family; for our variety of race and culture. We praise you that you did not create us to live in isolation but to share with others in loving relationships. Creator of us all,

We thank you.

Creator God, we thank you for your supreme gift in Jesus Christ; for his life on earth and oneness with the poor and outcast; for his dying and rising again to open new relationships; for gifts of choice and decision; for the ability to respond and be changed. Creator of Life,

We thank you.

Creator God, we thank you for family relationships here and now; for bonds of love that endure stress and strain; for mutual respect and the opportunity to develop our full potential; for the co-operation which makes us free to be ourselves and uphold our Christian values. Creator of feelings and sustainer of life,

We thank you.

Creator God, we thank you for continent and climate; for transport and travel; for the bonds of friendship and groups; for our fellowship with the family of the World Church; for the challenge and friendship of people of other faiths. Creator of all that is and shall be,

We thank you.

Rosemary Wass, United Kingdom

Thank you for people who laugh for tomorrow
because they are glad to have life for today.
Thank you for putting us into such a wonderful world
where there is so much to make us glad.

Helen Richards, Ireland

With thanksgiving we remember
the Spirit of God in the work of creation,
the Spirit alive in Christ's humanity,
the Spirit among us today,
inspiring and enabling us
to be partners in mission with God.

Anita Day, United Kingdom

Lord God, Creator of all, you gave birth
and clothed the earth with your splendour.
You filled it with colour and fragrance
and made it vibrate with music and sound,
perpetually swept by the movement of winds and clouds,
cleansed and renewed by rain and sunshine,
ever-changing scenes of light and darkness.
We are embraced with love and nurtured by all you provided.

You come to us on vast plains,
in the formation of rocks and stones,
on mountain tops and shaded woodland,
river, stream and lake,
illuminating everything with your presence,
renewing and making us whole.
We hear you in the sounds of water washing the shores,
the drone of insects,
the rustle of leaves and plants,
the voices of many creatures
and peoples of different languages
communicating together,
blending into one cosmic orchestra,
and, when all is quiet,
you are in the silence.

You made us fragile and vulnerable
and set us in an exciting,
changing and unpredictable world.
Like flowers and grass,
our physical bodies exist for a time
and return to dust.
Experiences of danger and suffering
reveal our dependence upon you
to lead us to what is reliable and enduring.
Creator God, your goodness is in everything.

Maureen Edwards

FOR OURSELVES

We bring you thanks, O God,
for our salvation through Christ,
for your bountiful creation:
rainfall, fertile land, sunshine -
when we use your resources wisely
we have enough and to spare.
For many years, the Church in our land
has shared the saving knowledge of Christ.
Help us still to employ our heads, hearts and hands
for human happiness and your glory.
May neighbours, through us, come to know your love.

Ghana

We give thanks for the diversity of languages and cultures
which enriches our common life, and pray for grace that we
may learn to live together in harmony.

Rajah Jacob, Sri Lanka

Lord, no one can tell what will happen
at the next rise above the crest of the waves.
We wonder why there is turbulence here and there.
We look up at the sky and see thin clouds break and fly past,
responding to an uprising storm in the far horizons.

No one knows why and how they all happen
and what they mean.
In trepidation and terror
we watch our shores
lest the high waters drown our beaches.

Lord, hasten the day when all creation is renewed,
with us,
in faith, hope and love.

Sione Amanaki Havea, Tonga

Let us pray that God will grant us the strength to participate with the oppressed in their struggle against injustice, debt and death; the wisdom to build bridges of friendship and unity, so that all the prejudices which separate people may be removed; the courage to protect, care and act responsibly within nature, and so recognise that we are part of the integrity of creation.

Lesley G Anderson, Panama

Lord we are all yours -
conceived in your mind long ages ago,
brought to birth through the patience of evolution,
redeemed by the love of Jesus.
Help us to realise the neighbourliness of creation.
Forgive us our desire to exploit and destroy.
Bring us to new horizons of kindness and service.
Restore in us reverence for all your works,
and teach us to call you our Father,
through Jesus, who is the pattern for us all.

Nigel Collinson, United Kingdom

Jesus brings peace
to all of us in the world;
he comes and unites us
because of our separation;
he breaks the barrier that separates our lives.

John Wesley Zinga, Solomon Islands

Supreme God of the universe, with your fullness you fill and sustain everything that is.
Beyond all form, giving form to all,
Recall us to your unity, Great God whom we adore.
With the touch of your hand,
you turn chaos to order,
darkness to light.
Unknown energies you hid in the heart of matter.
From you burst forth all energies.
Deep and wonderful are the mysteries of your creation.
Beyond all form, giving form to all,
Recall us to your unity, Great God whom we adore.

OCEANS OF PRAYER

You formed us in your image, creating us male and female.
You shape our union and harmony.
In this wondrous way you call us
to share the fullness of your own being,
your knowledge and your bliss.
Beyond all form, giving form to all,
Recall us to your unity, Great God whom we adore.
God of all salvation, through your Son,
who is the breaking in of your purpose in time and space,
you have shattered the walls
that divided us as man and woman.
In Christ you now show us there is no male or female.
Beyond all form, giving form to all,
Recall us to your unity, Great God whom we adore.

Eric Lott, India

God, your Son Jesus Christ has taught us
That Power belongs to you.
You have shared your power with us.
Yet, we confess
We have not accepted the power you have given us.
We have allowed others to use power
To dominate people and nations,
Exploiting them,
Creating wars,
And accumulating wealth.

Today you offer us your Power,
So that we can help change the world,
Announce your kingdom,
And acknowledge you,
The source of all power.
'For thine is the kingdom,
and the power,
and the glory,
for ever and ever'.

Diego Frisch, Uruguay

Lord Jesus Christ,
through whom and for whom,
the whole universe was created,
we mourn with you the death of forests,
fruitful lands that have become deserts,
wild animals left without grass,
plants, insects, birds and animals
threatened with extinction,
lands ravaged by war,
people left homeless.
As the earth cries out for liberation,
we confess our part in bringing it
towards the brink of catastrophe.
Through ignorance,
but often wilfully,
we thought we could serve God and mammon,
unable to resist the temptation
to spend and acquire more and more possessions,
with little thought of the consequences for future generations.
Saviour of the world, you call us to repentance:
to be transformed by your love,
deny ourselves,
take up the cross and follow in your way.

Maureen Edwards

Lord, we are sorry for being poor stewards of your creation.
You have given us a beautiful world and yet we have spoiled it
by greed and selfishness.
We have been slow to speak against the destruction of our
environment. We have unthinkingly let the politicians make
decisions for the future of our children. Forgive us.

Australia

Lord Jesus, open our eyes to see your glory and to see the world
as you see it; unstop our ears to hear your voice and to hear the
cries of the world as you hear them, in joys and sorrows; warm
our hearts with your love, that we may go to the world in your
name, and take your love to all in need, for your glory's sake.

Amos Cresswell, United Kingdom

Lord, you made us one people. In you, humankind is one family. Yet, in our blindness we have failed to recognise this unity.

Merciful God, forgive us.

We have emphasised divisions of sex, race and colour. We have tried to establish a scale of values based on such divisions.

Merciful God, forgive us.

We have created social and economic divisions within our own country and in the world at large. We have condemned some people to poverty and illiteracy while at the same time favouring others with the benefits of wealth and education.

Merciful God, forgive us.

God our Father, we are aware of your love and mercy. We know that in spite of our guilt, we are spared, individually and collectively, from carrying around our shortcomings like a heavy burden. Instead, we feel reassured when we hear your words which promise us pardon and freedom. Now with joy we receive the word of grace - our sins are forgiven.
We are free once more - free to love and serve you, Lord.

George and Elaine Mulrain, Caribbean

BEYOND OURSELVES

Dear God, may your Spirit live in us.
May the hot wind of the northern desert,
the cold wind from the South Pole,
the fresh breeze from the Pacific
bring us the power of your Spirit.
Help us to deepen the inner life
of our churches, in Chile and Britain:
make us one in your Spirit.
Help us to follow the ways of peace,
cherishing forgiveness and reconciliation.
Help us to be the voice of the poor
and powerless, who cannot express,
their huge needs and hidden hurt.
Help us to work for change,
with those who are oppressed.

Help us to do the work
of the ancient prophets in today's world.
We trust in your power, God,
but help us also to work hard.
We thank you for making us part
of your people, a network of caring covering the world.

Alicia Gutierrez, Chile

O heavenly Father, we praise you for your merciful protection.
You know, more than us, what is happening to us and our
country. We know that the way we live exploits others and
degrades your creation. May your Holy Spirit enlighten
political leaders and guide us all to respect human rights and
the living world. May life be renewed, may your name be
magnified.

Valentin Dedji, Benin

Father, in your creation you have made us rich,
And yet we have made ourselves poor
In our reluctance to credit others with value;
In our failure to look beyond the material and accepted
standards of our day;
In our deafness to hear only the sounds that are pleasant to our
ears;
In our noise and business, failing to listen
to the unuttered cries of hurt and pain;
In our lifestyle putting the pleasure of palate
before the real cost to individuals in another part of the world.

We live as though our well-being matters most
And because of that, the rest of creation suffers.
Father, forgive us.
Help us to visualise your values,
To appreciate your resources,
But above all to credit all humankind as members of the family,
Valuable and indispensable.

Rosemary Wass, United Kingdom

OCEANS OF PRAYER

Our Lord, God! We pray for people whose farms are barren and those whose homes have been swept away by floods. They are living every day with despair and hopelessness but believe in the Lord who has power to change impossible into possible.

Our merciful Lord, lead them through the floods.

We pray for the farmers who belong to the land and the land belongs to them. They plough it. Their hands become coarse. Their sweat runs down their bodies and into the earth to give fruitful crops to be enjoyed by all people of the earth and mostly by those who never dirty their hands.

Our merciful Lord! Open our hearts to seek justice for them. Save us from the temptation to enjoy better living standards at the cost of increased poverty for others.

We pray for those who have one small shanty room as their home for the whole family. They get along very well with animals who share the same court yard and accept each other's right of possession. While the parents work hard to maintain the family, the children are left alone.

Our Creator, help us remember that Jesus did speak for the weak and gave them a message of hope. Help us to accept his calling to work for the weak and oppressed.

Pakistan

O God, save our shores from the weapons of death,
our lands from things that deny our young ones love and freedom.
Let the seas carry messages of peace and goodwill.
Turn away from our midst any unkind and brutal practices.
Let each child swim and breathe the fresh air
that is filled by the Holy Spirit.
O Lord Jesus, bless all who are makers of that peace
that breaks down the barriers of hatred,
and unite us with the open arms of your cross,
that all the peoples of the world may live happily together.

Sione Amanaki Havea, Tonga

Strengthen us, Lord, by the power of your Holy Spirit, that our dreams of a society where men and women are equal, where all share what they have and live with justice and love, that these dreams may be realised in our time, through Jesus Christ our Lord.

Rajah Jacob, Sri Lanka

Our Father
whose will encompasses heaven and earth,
your world offers home and living space for all of us.
We bring before you
the needs of those who find no rest and home in the world,
who lack the things mostly needed for their lives,
or become ill because of an ill world.
We pray for those who live in super-cities
and in tents for refugees,
in the areas of drought and flood,
for all who live in places where the trees are dying.

Let us realise, that we have to shape
and take care of the world which came from your hands
for us and our children.
We call upon you:

Lord, hear our prayer.

Our Father,
To whom we turn for bread day by day,
Your creative power has provided food for everybody.
We remember our sisters and brothers
who ask you - as we do -
for their daily bread,
the cup of rice,
the blanket for the night
- and receive nothing.
Let us realise where we have failed to help them
and where our affluence has caused their poverty.
Let us repent, that there might be help for them
and ourselves
so that together we may give thanks to you
for everything that you are giving, each day anew.
We call upon you:

Lord, hear our prayer.

OCEANS OF PRAYER

Our Father,
whom we ask to forgive our sins:
We are allowed to live together
as people who are reconciled in you.
Therefore we need to respond, with anger and tears
to any cruelty and violence,
any unkindness and oppression,
whether we are the victims,
whether we are only the spectators,
or we are the perpetrators.
Teach us to live together in such a way,
that our neighbours here and abroad
will not be cheated of their rights.
Let us not only look after our own interest
and thus trespass against them.
Teach us justice which brings about true peace.
We call upon you:

Lord, hear our prayer.

Our Father,
whose kingdom and power and glory we praise:
In your son Jesus Christ
you offered to us the fullness of life.
We are ashamed in the light of your promises.
How inadequate is the response of our love and fellowship.
How seldom your kingdom and your glory,
for which we long,
become reality.
Make us new through your spirit!
Let us serve you in your church and reflect your glory
that the world may know the things that make for peace.
We call upon you:

Lord, hear our prayer.

Dr Ruediger Minor, Germany

MEDITATIONS

Look at these birds:
they feed on flowers,
they peck at insects,
pick up seeds.
They have no house,
they have no home,
they roost in the trees.
God cares for them.
Look at these birds,
God cares for them,
who is father and mother to you.

Look at these flowers,
splendid creatures,
idle beauties,
content to bloom.
They grow, they bud,
they blossom fair.
They have no care;
God cares for them.
Look at these flowers,
God cares for them,
who is father and mother to you.

More than the birds,
more than the flowers,
though Solomon's robes
cannot compare,
nor human voice
can match these birds':
more than them all,
God cares for you,
more than them all,
God cares for you,
who is father and mother to you.

Why do you worry?
Food and drink,
a roof and clothes,
and all you need;
your children too,
their health and school,
God cares for them.
He cares for you.
Why do you worry?
God cares for you,
who is father and mother to you.

Hugh Thomas, United Kingdom

OCEANS OF PRAYER

We believe that Creation is a gift of God, an expression of our Creator's goodness.
We believe that the resources of our lands and waters and air are precious gifts from our Creator, to be used and looked after with loving care.
We believe that there is a rhythm to God's creation, like a drum beat. When we lose the beat, or the drum is damaged, the music is out of tune.
We believe that as Christians, we are called to be peacemakers, in order that our world and our communities, and each person may experience the true peace which God promises us.
We believe that this may sometimes mean 'disturbing the peace', as Jesus did, for a purpose - to restore the purpose of God.
We believe that our Pacific ways are also a gift from God. We are invited to use the values of our Pacific cultures to build societies of justice and peace.

The Pacific

The Earth is the Lord's - but he's given it to us
to rule over, have dominion, subdue,
to use, develop, exploit.
Throughout the world, this attitude prevails,
The Earth is the Lord's - but we can improve it.
Drain the marshes, clear the scrub,
level the hills, fill in ponds,
make new lakes, build new mountains,
excavate new valleys, create new wastelands,
build on green fields, concrete jungle,
civilise the primitive, eliminate the elements.

The Earth is the Lord's - but he's given it to us.
To rule over, have dominion, subdue,
to use, develop, exploit.
Close to the earth, this attitude prevails -
The Earth is the Lord's - but we can improve it.
Maximise output - whatever the inputs,
fertilizer, fungicide, herbicide, insecticide,
growth promotion and growth regulation,
nature controlled with the contents of a bottle.
Simplify, streamline, specialise,
efficiency - economy of sale.
Enlarge the fields for yet bigger machines.
Merge the farms and lose the farmers.

And what of God's creatures?
He's given them to us,
to rule over, have dominion, subdue.
Warm and comfortable - but captive,
high stocking density, detached from daylight,
no room to flap, no dust to bathe,
life sustained by constant medication,
increased production, rapid turnover.
We all reap the benefit, food is cheap,
justice and gentleness have a higher price.

The Earth is the Lord's - but we make demands,
a newer car, a bigger car, an extra car.
Three-lane motorways -
freedom to choose and freedom to move.
More heat, more light - we can pay the price,
disposable income on disposable goods.
Maximum life for minimum effort,
the earth pays the true cost,
and groans in agony.

But the Earth is the Lord's - not ours at all,
not ours to abuse and exhaust,
not ours to poison and plunder,
not ours to lay waste and abandon,
but God's, to be cared for and cherished.

What arrogance we display - what games we play,
what profits we gain.
Buying and selling, trading and speculating,
but the Earth is the Lord's, not ours at all!

Howard Wass, United Kingdom

Come to the world!
Yes, God the Creator, come!
Things are not as you created them in the beginning.
Come, God, for it is your help we need in the world.

Peace of mind,
Yes, that's what everyone wants.
Our need, please God, is true peace in the world.
Peace of mind,
Yes, that's what everyone prays for.

What is our state in the world?
Come and see how our people are destroying the world,
without seeking what is in your heart,
without seeking what is in your mind.
Come and see how retaliation prevails among us,
without fearing you,
without recognising brotherhood.

Rise, brethren and live together,
for it will be well.
Yes, if we seek peace,
God will grant us peace.
Peace, brethren, it is unity
the mercy of God,
peace and purity of heart,
that will raise us up.

Let all persons ask themselves,
'What is our role among the people of the world?'
It is peace,
that encourages the heart;
and making peace
that is the guarantee of hope.

Ikole Harcourt Whyte, Nigeria

Reflecting on Luke 4.14-20

The prophecy of Isaiah continues to be fulfilled:
in the favelas of South America,
where hope and dignity are given in poverty;
in leprosy settlements in Nigeria,
where respect and love are shared;
in the striving for justice in South Africa,
the Philippines and Haiti;

in all the loving, caring service in nursery groups,
day care centres for the elderly,
work with the mentally and physically handicapped;
in projects for the unemployed;

in countless areas in the world,
the love and power of God bring change and hope.

The love of God is alive in the world.
God's power is the power of love:
love freely given,
painfully given,
joyfully given,
abundantly given,
and love gives power to change.

Anne Knighton, United Kingdom

The Stranger

There was more, far more than I knew,
to my sky.
The sky I knew
lay above my roof-tops
and I thought I knew
every star in my sky.
But you came, stranger,
and told me of other roof-tops, other skies.
You showed me other stars
and a country without frontiers
of which I knew nothing.

There was more, far more than I knew,
to my earth.
The gardens I knew
were full of apple-trees and cherries.
But you came, stranger,
and planted my garden
with palms and olive plants,
and showed me a force in the earth
of which I knew nothing.

There was more, far more than I knew
to my tongue.
My tongue used to sing
in its own special accent and dialect.
But you came, stranger,
with other sounds,
and new words,
and taught me songs
of which I knew nothing.

OCEANS OF PRAYER

There was more, far more than I knew
to my skin.
Down my street have come people
of every hue
from ebony black to golden brown.
And you came, stranger,
opening up limitless horizons
and astonishing countries
of which I knew nothing.

There was a whole world on my doorstep.
You,
and others,
and God.
A whole world of which I knew nothing.

John Pritchard, United Kingdom

Renewed Communities in Love

INTRODUCTION

Community is one of those words enjoying a comeback in everyday use. We are told that the needs of the disabled, the deprived and the elderly would be better met by 'community care' than by the old social institutions. We are advised that 'community service' would be a better remedy for delinquency than imprisonment. And the new system of financing local facilities is called 'community charge' rather than the less popular term 'poll tax'. But communities do not come into being simply as a convenient social arrangement. They are born out of shared experience and grow best in a climate of love.

From its earliest days, the Church was a community of people drawn together by their common experience of the love of God and sharing their lives and their livelihood in a relationship of love towards one another. That love became a closer bond than ties of kith or kin or even cultural tradition. Jew and Gentile, bond and free, male and female discovered that, in Christ, the differences that had once separated them became a diversity that enriched their unity.

In our own times, when divisive forces of sectarianism, nationalism and racism are among the most perilous threats to world peace, the Gospel of Christ calls us to pray that locally, nationally and globally, we may break down the barriers, open up new corridors of service and share our resources, firmly believing that it is God's purpose that we dwell as one loving community in his one world.

Pauline Webb, United Kingdom

PRESENCE

Lord, as we worship today give us vision.
Move us by your Spirit.
Bring good news to us all.
Freedom to broken people.
And Heaven, here on Earth.
Open our eyes to see you as you really are,
and open our hearts to praise you.

Give us a vision that will carry us through
our disappointments and our failures,
our anxious and unhappy times,
and the monotony of boring routines.

Give us a vision that will lift our lives
and lead us to new ways of service.

Help us to dare to dream of love
in a world that speaks of hate.

Help us to dare to dream of hope
in a world that speaks of despair.

Help us to dare to dream of peace
in a world that speaks of war.

In our worship today, Lord, give us vision
through Jesus Christ our Lord.

United Kingdom

Jesus, we come to you
seeking to know more surely
how to live, how to take our place
in this, your world.

Dear Lord, feed us with the living bread.

Like people of old in Galilee,
we are full of questions and make demands.
So show us first that you know best
what is just and lovely and true.

Dear Lord, feed us with the living bread.

Show us the Kingdom of God that means
release for the captives and sight for the blind;
release of body, mind and spirit;
release for us and for those we despise
or fear or hate.

Dear Lord, feed us with the living bread.

Help us all
to know the truth that makes us free.
Satisfy those deeper needs
of body, mind and spirit
we have not recognised
either in ourselves or in others.

Dear Lord, feed us with the living bread.

In the company of your disciples,
where we belong,
nourish us, build us up
in fullness of life.
Let us grow together,
in faith and love and service,
more like you.

Dear Lord, feed us with the living bread.

Hugh Thomas, United Kingdom

PRAISE AND THANKSGIVING

Lord God, our heavenly Father,
we thank you for the peoples of this part of the world,
with all their rich variety.
We thank you for the followers
of Jesus Christ in these lands
who are called in the midst of such diversity
to bear witness to those qualities of life
that transcend all barriers.
Pour your Holy Spirit on your Church
that she may be a transforming power
for reconciliation, unity and peace.

Rajah Jacob, Sri Lanka

Lord we thank you
For our history and the outpouring of power and devotion
Through a flood of people who found you.

For all who have followed them;
Pastors, preachers, teachers and faithful witnesses
Living stones built into a spiritual house.

For institutions, for all who serve them
And all whom they serve:
Some to prepare kindly homes
Some to foster health and wholeness
Some to battle for minds and hearts and lives.

For people from many lands
Joining with the people of the land
To shape a unity of will and spirit
Informing a body of growing strength.

So now, on their foundation,
We look to the future in hope and confidence
Placing ourselves in your hands.

We do not seek independence
But to be dependent on you
And then on one another.

Fashion us one people
For your work
Of reconciling, renewing, creating love.

Côte d'Ivoire

We are one world-wide family in Christ. We give thanks for
people in every generation who have shared this vision and
responded to God's call to serve overseas, remembering
especially pioneers who willingly faced dangers of travel,
climate, disease and persecution to fulfil their calling.

Lord, we thank you we are one family in Christ.

Let us thank God for those who were missionaries in their own
lands: for their courage in answering Christ's call and facing
persecution by their own people.

Lord, we thank you we are one family in Christ.

OCEANS OF PRAYER

Let us praise God for the work of the World Church today: for the development and growth of national Church leadership.

Lord, we thank you we are one family in Christ.

Let us thank God for our partnership in mission throughout the world; for those who go overseas and for those who come as missionaries to Britain to enrich our faith.

Lord, we thank you we are one family in Christ.

Elizabeth Bellamy, United Kingdom

We thank you, God
Because you give us
more than we would ever dream of asking:
daily bread and shared meals that become feasts,
the breath of life, and voices to celebrate,
the understanding of our history and the hope of our future.
Work we can do, and time to be recreated,
people to love and trust,
people who love and trust us,
gifts and responsibilities.
We thank you, God
because you ask of us
more than we dream of giving:
skills we have never developed,
care for a world whose problems we cannot solve,
listening which hurts us,
giving which leaves us empty handed,
love which makes us vulnerable,
faith which seems impossible.
But you do not ask us to be supermen and women.
You challenge us to be human.
Give us the courage to be human
because you yourself became human
and lived our lives,
knowing our imperfections,
sharing our joy and pain,
making us your people
so that we can say together,
'Our Father . . .'

Jan S Pickard

O God, we thank you
for the different expressions of your way in different cultures.
May your Church go on growing and changing
in response to the gospel,
to our shared traditions and the needs of the people.
May its ministers be true servants;
may its gifts be shared for the good of all;
may communication open minds and hearts;
may your children, within and without the church,
be reconciled;
together may we experience revival.

Nigeria

Caring God, you come to us as Mother and Father, revealing
the many facets of your love in the traditions of all peoples. The
world is large but you are larger, able to work by the Spirit's
power in every place. Thank you for making us part of something much greater and very wonderful, loved members of an
extended and varied family. Make us one in your love.

United Kingdom

Lighten our darkness, Lord, we pray:
that we and all your people
may learn to deal justly, love mercy
and walk humbly with you
and with each other.
Let the continents praise you from shore to shore,
with drum and song and dance,
in freedom, love and sharing.

John Pritchard, United Kingdom

FOR OURSELVES

Father you have revealed yourself to us,
by all means,
in every experience of life,
and supremely in your son Jesus Christ.
You have provided us richly
with every good gift
of time, money and skills.
We offer ourselves -
a living sacrifice,
ready for service and mission
in your world.
Give us grace,
that by all means,
we share your gospel of new life
with everyone.

Maureen Edwards

Lord God,
we believe that your revelation comes to every nation
in its real and concrete situation;
Help us to see you more clearly in our tradition and culture.
Lord God, we believe that you have called us
to be your hands and feet in this land.
Help us to be living witnesses
of your love and grace to all people.
Lord God we believe you are the king of the universe.
May your justice and peace reign among us.

Charles Klagba, Togo

We see ourselves, O God,
people of faith and faithlessness -
dancing in the sun one day
and overwhelmed by our realities on the next,
joyfully announcing the gospel sometimes
and then trembling in our uncertainty.
We see the hope that lies among us -
and hope that we could care
and live in community with each other
and the world.

Australia

For beauty and gentleness we praise you, O Father,
For challenge and testing we submit to you, O Father,
For victory over self and sin we pray you, O Father.

Tonga

Let us admit to God, and to one another,
where we have failed him and his Church:
we are reluctant to accept change and receive new ideas.
We allow ourselves to feel threatened by what seems strange.
Our conservatism runs deep,
even among young people.

Forgive us, healer and reconciler.

We tend to be clergy-centred,
leaving many people uncared for,
even though we have the gifts and skills to serve them.
We have failed to heed the challenge of Paul
that those who are leaders must exert themselves to lead.

Forgive us, healer and reconciler.

We allow political and economic ideologies
to divide us in Church and society.
Our selfishness and greed create and maintain barriers
of increasing wealth and debilitating poverty.

Forgive us, healer and reconciler.

Herbie McGhie, Caribbean

For those whom you have called, we give praise.
Though on earth by sin and tribulations beset,
They yet found guidance enough to give you praise,
As they at all times felt by your love beset.

Gracious Lord of the Church militant and triumphant,
Help us declare your fatherly justice and mercy,
Until, by your grace, all, who may, join the triumphant,
who now live in the fulfilment of your justice and mercy.

Crispin Mazobere, Zimbabwe

OCEANS OF PRAYER

Grandfather, look at our brokenness.
We know that in all creation only the human family
has strayed from the sacred way.
We know that we are the ones who are divided
and we are the ones who must come back together
to walk in the sacred way.
Grandfather, Sacred One,
teach us love, compassion and honour
that we may heal the earth and heal each other.

North America

Our Father God, Creator of all your different children
all that has come to be has come through you,
lives in your energy,
takes breath because you willed it,
is clothed in your beauty and dignity,
valued and loved by you, Father,
and is part of your world.

Our Father, God, Creator of all your different children,
teach us to love what you have created.
Help us to shed the arrogance that cocoons us
and restricts our growth.
Help us to split the binding threads of self
that we may crawl out into the warmth of your light,
borne on the wings of understanding.
Teach us to see people one by one
and to acknowledge them as our Father's children,
our brothers and sisters:
not to pigeonhole them;
not to hammer them into unnatural moulds
of our own making,
but to rejoice in our differences,
accepting people as they are
- different but of equal worth -
each one a part of God's creation,
showing something of his love and glory.

Sybil Phoenix, United Kingdom

We pray that we may live in unity with everyone who confesses the same holy name and who accepts the same Gospel.
Father of us all, unite us.
May we not turn away from the world and never turn on each other in fear and mistrust.
The Gospel can be a stick in our hand to lean upon, or even to strike out. We pray that the Gospel may be an extended hand for the world.
O God, teach us that the Gospel of Jesus Christ never discriminates, never refuses, never condemns. May all Christians live in truth and love.

Martin Beukenhorst, Belgium

Lord, since the fellowship meal of the Messiah will not begin until the whole human family is able to sit around the royal banquet table, and because to wait for one another, especially those who are weak and heavy-laden, is to name your name, O God, help us to be patient with others, so that we may truly pray, 'Give us this day our daily bread'.

I S Tuwere, the Pacific

Lord, you come to us but we do not recognise you;
you call but we do not follow;
you command but we do not obey,
you bless us but we do not thank you.

Please forgive and help us.

Lord, you accept us but we do not accept others;
you forgive us but we do not forgive those who wrong us;
you love us but we do not love our neighbours.

Please forgive and help us.

Lord, you showed us how to carry out our mission,
but we still insist on our own;
you identified yourself with outcasts, the needy and
the poor,
but we do not bother to find out what is happening to them;
you suffered and died for the sake of all,
but we do not give up our comfortable lives.

Please forgive and help us.

Bernie Colorado, the Philippines

OCEANS OF PRAYER

Lord Jesus Christ,
you are alive in the world:
among the poor and oppressed,
the pavement dwellers
and refugees
of Africa, Asia
and Latin America . . .
Amid the garbage and ruins,
in depths of despair and suffering,
there you are.
The friendly face of a homeless child
stares up at us;
an old man smiles and blesses us;
a beggar woman shares a handful of rice
between her hungry children
and the orphan who joins them.
Of such is the Kingdom.

Lord Jesus Christ,
we cannot see you as Thomas did,
nor touch you with our hands,
but you come in unexpected ways
and speak through people
whose background and outlook
are different from our own.
Help us to listen with respect
to their experience
and reflect upon their insights.
Free us from pride
to find your dignity and presence
wherever you are.

Maureen Edwards

Father, who formed the human family to live in harmony and
peace, we acknowledge before you our divisions, quarrels,
hatreds, injustices and greed. May your Church demonstrate
before the world the power of the Gospel to destroy division, so
that, in Christ Jesus, there may be no barriers of wealth or class,
age or intellect, race or colour, but all may be equally your
children, members one of another and heirs together of your
everlasting Kingdom.

Nigeria

May our partnership become deeper:
May we pool our resources
of money, people and talents;
May we share what we have learned
of unity and spirituality,
experience and practicality;
May we stand together
to show the world the love of God
which can overcome the hatred
and division in the world,
if we are true to our calling as the Church.

J E Ghose, North India

May new avenues of service open for us and may we grow
closer to one another in the love of the Lord.

Zimbabwe

May God give us new visions,
to take advantage of new possibilities,
to go out and reach new people.
May the Holy Spirit empower us to do this work.

Josef Ceruenak, Czechoslovakia

Lord Jesus Christ, you showed us how to relate to one another
when you washed the feet of those who were your friends and
partners in mission. Teach us now that true discipleship
depends not on feelings but following, not on ecstasy but
obedience, and may we discover the joy that comes from
serving and listening to one another.

United Kingdom

We offer ourselves
to work in partnership with you,
Father, Son and Holy Spirit,
in our homes
and in the mission of your Church.
Enlarge our vision of the world
and give us the stamina
to make it a reality
to your glory!

United Kingdom

OCEANS OF PRAYER

We, who receive so much from a generous God,
who are shown life fully lived in Jesus,
who know perfect love in his sacrificial death,
who share resurrection joy in his rising again,
bring our offerings, tokens of our love and
unity in your service.

Kate Johnson, United Kingdom

God our Father, grant to your people a deeper confidence in your power, and an expectancy that the Church's life and mission will grow stronger, for the sake of Jesus Christ and the world he came to save.

Roger Ducker, United Kingdom

At our stations or in study
At home or abroad
May God keep us joyous
And faithful in the task
That the Holy Spirit guides us to do.

Donald C Henry, Caribbean

Lord, we are willing to face the challenge
of mission and discipleship,
even when this means the personal sacrifice
of energy, time and possessions.

Lord, you called us and now we come,
you commanded us and now we go,
you taught us your will and now we obey.

And, as you promised, Lord,
we know that we will not be alone
in our journey of faith and mission,
for you are always with us.

Bernie Colorado, the Philippines

O God our Father, we pray for the wisdom, grace and power of the Holy Spirit upon our Church leaders, so that the Church may venture forth in faith with the Gospel of love and be driven out to fill the country with peace and justice.

Harold Fernando, Sri Lanka

Give us grace, O Lord, committed to Christ, to seize the present opportunity; and, empowered by your Spirit, to look to the future with expectation. Help us to love, listen and learn, to offer and proclaim, so that boys and girls, men and women, may come to the joy of your service.

Kenneth S J Hext, United Kingdom

Let us try to imagine the worldwide Church as God wants it to be. Picture it in its strength and power - the effect it would have on the world.

(Silence)

Father, fill your Church with love and power, that together we may change the world

- and Lord, may it start with me.

Let us imagine our Church here in . . . . as God would want it to be.

(Silence)

Father, this is your Church. We are your workers here on earth. Guide us, show us, lead us, make us as we ought to be

- and Lord, may it start with me.

Let us try to imagine ourselves as God would like us to be - whole and perfect, full of love, joy, hope and peace.

(Silence)

Lord, all things are possible with you. Fill us with your spirit that we may fulfil all that you want us to be. Lord - let love fill the world

- and Lord, may it start with me.

Gillian Weeks, United Kingdom

BEYOND OURSELVES

Son of the carpenter, enable all young people with vision, courage, confidence and skills; may they live productive lives with their self-worth and dignity enhanced; may they become useful citizens in their country and living stones in the house of God; unite us all in you, the chief cornerstone, the same Jesus Christ our Lord.

Bill Watty, Caribbean

Loving God, we pray for
the poor, hungry, the uprooted
and those who do not know where they are going -
may the church be good news to them;
for tourists and travellers who come in touch with the church
- may they hear the Gospel;
for those who are sick or in sorrow
- may they know the care of the church;
for those who care, ministers and medical workers
- may they find strength, support and times of stillness;
for students of all kinds,
in schools, ministerial training,
people learning the skills of nursing or farming
- may they grow in the knowledge of God.

Kenya

Lord of all nations, from your Word we learn of your plan to bring people of every kind into one family. You have no favourite and love each and every person with total love. We remember again that you made us of one blood and that all divisions which separate your people from one another stand over against your kingly rule.

We pray earnestly for this country and her varied peoples. We give thanks for the witness of the Churches through many years to the unity of your family. We pray that your Holy Spirit may find entrance to minds that are darkened by prejudice and closed by fears of others.

Bring calmness of mind and clarity of vision to those who have leadership responsibility. May we learn again the meaning of mission in Christ's Way.

Rajah Jacob, Sri Lanka

O God, we acknowledge the sin of racism. We have not been what you have called us to be. We have wounded the body of Christ even as we have wounded those persons whom you have called to share in your grace. Forgive us our sin and lead us into new life through the one who was broken for us.

Sybil Phoenix, United Kingdom

May your Church now, blessed Lord Jesus, through your Holy Spirit, bear witness throughout the world and our own society to your power to change, your ability to transform, your compassion to renew, your comfort to relieve, your love to forgive, and ministry to reconcile.

Lesley G Anderson, Panama

Dear Lord,
fill your church with love and understanding, so that she may show forth your gospel love.

In your name we pray.

Fill your people with respect for each other, a willingness to listen and a generosity to share.

In your name we pray.

Enable us to listen to and help all who suffer through injustice and neglect.

In your name we pray.

May those with skill and understanding, with knowledge and intellect be so guided by your love, that they harness their power for the good of all.

In your name we pray.

May those who suffer in pain, distress, loneliness and grief know the power of your healing love.

In your name we pray.

May we, in all we do and say, in all we are and strive to be, be filled with your loving power.

In your name we pray.

Anne Knighton, United Kingdom

OCEANS OF PRAYER

Almighty God, Father, Son and Holy Spirit,
we give you thanks for who you are.
We remember with thankful hearts
the liberating power of the Gospel,
the light that has become ours
through faithful messengers of past, present and future;
the illuminating power of the Holy Spirit
through whom Christ has become one of us.

We pray for the Church, both local and universal,
to be serious and urgent with the Gospel,
that the people of all ages
will know the need to share Christ with others.
That youth will feel part of the whole Church -
full members with rights and responsibilities,
that your work may continue through us.

Albert Burua, Papua New Guinea

Loving God, we pray for all who witness to you in schools, colleges and universities, that in the face of many different ideologies, Christ's loving influence may shine forth upon young lives. We pray for the many young people who are becoming increasingly frustrated because they are unemployed. Give them the power to discern what is your will for their lives. Lord, in your mercy:

Hear our prayer.

Loving God, we pray for all who exercise political leadership and influence, that they may become more dedicated to the creation of one family on earth. We pray for the Church, that in its mission it may also seek to further the cause of unity among all peoples, acknowledging this as yet another step towards the establishment of God's Kingdom upon earth. Lord, in your mercy:

Hear our prayer.

Lord you have received prayers of concern for the world. We are conscious of the fact that we often hold the key to many of the world's problems. So accept us now as we offer ourselves afresh to you, fully determined to serve you in whatever way you ask. May your Holy Spirit move in us so that our lives are a daily involvement in the mission to which Christ has called us. Lord, in your mercy:

Hear our prayer.

George and Elaine Mulrain, Caribbean

May those who profess Christianity be firmly rooted and grounded in their faith; may they withstand the pressures of spurious teaching, and no longer be tossed hither and thither by every wind of doctrine.

Wycherley Gumbs, Caribbean

Give us strength to build evermore bridges of peace all over the world.

Tonga

Fire of the Spirit -
moving and loving -
warm us and lead us,
encourage and change us.

Fire of the Spirit -
give light to our chaos,
drive out our confusions
and heal our hurt world.

Fire of the Spirit -
join us together,
dance in our churches,
transform our lives.

Jan S Pickard

Keep your Church free, that it may be the channel through which justice and peace, integrity and wholeness, harmony and good will, may flow to the dispossessed and the desperate, that your Kingdom may come in all its fulfilment of life and health and peace, through Jesus Christ our Lord.

Jamaica

MEDITATIONS

To church on Sunday,
to gabled stone or patched thatched mud-walled chapels;
in suits, in colourful cloth, immaculate choir robes or tatters;
for fervent prayer and full-throated song.
On Monday meeting, greeting on the road
by market stall, or well, or river's bank;
tilling the fields, and watching for the rain
- 'To plant, or not to plant, that is the question' -
sowing in faith, harvesting joy?
Or tears?
Others to school: children of all ages, in outsize classes
bookless, chalkless, even benchless;
yet neatly uniformed, bright-eyed, eager,
and teachers, variously trained
or untrained: heroes, heroines and miracle-workers.
And some with burdens, not of wood or water,
but policies, decisions, responsibilities,
nation-builders, leaders of the people.
While some meet once again to sing and pray,
laying their dead to rest:
the scarcely-born, the prematurely old.
Blessed are those who mourn,
for they have many comforters,
sitting with them at home, sharing their sorrow,
then gathering grieving at the grave.
On Tuesday, and the whole week long,
they live their daily lives
in comfort or discomfort,
advantaged or deprived,
remembering perhaps last Sunday's sermon,
or preparing for the next . . .
Mothers and fathers, elders and youngsters, typists, shop-
keepers, farmers,
in ambling ox-carts, crowded buses, chauffeur-driven cars,
making money, love, trouble, peace,
our sisters and brothers, Christ's followers in Africa,
calling for our prayers
and praying for us.

John Pritchard, United Kingdom

The native elders speak at great length about the circle of life:
there is a place in the circle for everyone. There is no exclusion.
Our futures are bound together, part of the whole global
community.

Stanley McKay, Canada

Still shining surface
of the lake;
so much beauty,
so much power
locked up
beneath the glassy cover;
so many drops of water
indistinguishable;
let fall one spot
of rain
and here's a miracle;
the glass is shattered,
ring upon ring
pushed outwards
bounding to the shore
and back again,
like the people of God
joyful,
driven by him
into the world.

But here's another spot
and another;
spot after spot,
circle after circle,
backwards and forwards,
crossing, creating,
pulsing patterns,
glittering light
and liquid laughter,
giving and taking,
change and exchange;
from a million congregations
intertwined;
the lake a dancing glory,
the world aflame.

Betty Hares, United Kingdom

OCEANS OF PRAYER

Lord, here I am, a stranger in a strange land;
a foreigner, a guest,
whose skin makes me stand out,
arousing suspicion, resentment, alienation.

Lord, watch my steps, lest I cause offence;
give me grace to recognise when I go wrong;
pick me up each time I stumble.
Make me watchful of the eyes of those I meet,
that I may be alert to any shaft of anger;
recognise the look that reveals a lack of mutual understanding;
respond with my own eyes to welcome and to laughter.

Give me a mind curious to learn,
so that I may listen intently
to what is being said beneath the words that are spoken;
listen with humility
when my race and customs are being criticised;
listen with patience,
knowing that I am only beginning
to understand all that there is to learn
from this people and their culture.

Lord, I am a stranger, yet still I am at home;
at home with my brothers and sisters in Christ;
at home where I meet with them in worship,
even though I do not know each word they use;
at home as I share with them the bread that is your body,
the wine that is your blood,
dissolving all the differences of race and tongue,
class and custom,
wealth and education;
reconciling all wrongs done by one nation to another;
liberating us from all our past.
For in you we are all one,
and nothing can separate us from the love of Christ.

David Temple, United Kingdom

The prophet Ezekiel
shared the suffering
of his people
exiled in Babylon,
ridiculed,
discriminated against,
resented,
a minority group.
Their community broken,
their hope destroyed,
they looked like
a valley of dry bones,
disconnected,
lifeless,
ineffective.
Yet he saw
in the future
God breathing into them,
covering them with flesh,
sinews and skin.
A whole army of living people
rose up out of the valley.
A community had come alive!
Each bone,
limb and person,
essentially different,
had become one people
celebrating
and enjoying life together.

This is the word of God!
God's Spirit moves among our differences
to bring us together
into a living community!

Maureen Edwards

OCEANS OF PRAYER

We are the branches of the vine.
Branches grow and move.
Each leaf has the space it needs
To be itself, to give of itself
To build the plant.

We are the branches of the vine.
Not leaves or flowers
that fade or fall.
But branches, determining the shape
In relation to the stem.

We are branches of the vine.
The supporting trellis stands
Well preserved, immune to change,
Destined to rot.
Each branch so fragile, so vulnerable
Growing through change.

We are the branches of the vine.
The stem will never fruit.
The health of the plant
Will always be measured
By the fruit of the branches.

David Cowling, United Kingdom